REESE RYAN

A VALENTINE FOR CHRISTMAS

HARLEQUIN®
DESIRE™

Recycling programs
for this product may
not exist in your area.

ISBN-13: 978-1-335-58152-5

A Valentine for Christmas

Harlequin Enterprises ULC
22 Adelaide St. West, 41st Floor
Toronto, Ontario M5H 4E3, Canada
www.Harlequin.com

Printed in U.S.A.

Reese Ryan writes sexy, emotional love stories served with a heaping side of family drama.

Reese is a native Ohioan with deep Tennessee roots. She endured many long, hot car trips to family reunions in Memphis via a tiny clown car loaded with cousins.

Connect with Reese via Facebook, Twitter, Instagram, TikTok or reeseryan.com. Join her VIP Readers Lounge at bit.ly/VIPReadersLounge. Check out her YouTube show, where she chats with fellow authors, at bit.ly/ReeseRyanChannel.

Books by Reese Ryan

Harlequin Desire

The Bourbon Brothers

Savannah's Secrets
The Billionaire's Legacy
Engaging the Enemy
A Reunion of Rivals
Waking Up Married
The Bad Boy Experiment

Valentine Vineyards

A Valentine for Christmas

Visit her Author Profile page at Harlequin.com, or reeseryan.com, for more titles.

You can find Reese Ryan on Facebook, along with other Harlequin Desire authors, at Facebook.com/harlequindesireauthors!

My new Valentine Vineyards series is dedicated to everyone who has read my Bourbon Brothers series and taken the Abbott family into their hearts. Because you weren't quite ready to let go of Joe, Duke, Iris, Blake, Parker, Max, Cole and Zora Abbott or end our adventures in Magnolia Lake, neither was I.

I hope you'll enjoy getting to know the Valentines and their regular interactions with the growing Abbott family.

One

Chandra Valentine gripped the handle of her rolling carry-on luggage as she watched the tiny regional plane taxi toward her gate at the Charlotte Douglas International Airport. She honestly wished she hadn't seen it. Then she could pretend it was a larger plane. A stable plane. The kind she'd become accustomed to flying in over her past thirty-nine years of life. Not one of those little puddle jumpers she'd always taken great pains to avoid.

She loosened her grip when she realized her nails were stabbing her palms. She opened her hand, studying the row of angry semicircles that trailed across her skin. Chandra took a deep breath, her eyes drifting closed momentarily. When she opened them, she was greeted by a penetrating dark gaze.

The incredibly handsome man tipped his chin in

greeting as he rubbed his full beard. Typically, she'd considered a full-grown beard a turnoff. Who knew exactly what might be lurking in that thing? But for this brother, she'd make an exception.

He was dressed in an unbuttoned, green-and-black plaid shirt over a black Henley shirt, distressed jeans and brown Timberland boots. His lopsided smile made her belly flip in ways it hadn't in longer than she cared to admit.

Chandra gave him a quick nod and an awkward wave before sauntering away.

The man was *fine*. In ways she could wax poetically about for days. But this wasn't a girls' trip to Vegas. She was about to board a tuna can with wings so she could meet her dad in some small mountain town in Tennessee.

If she didn't feel a sense of urgency to get to the little town of Magnolia Lake, where her dad had summoned her and her five younger siblings, she would've flown to the closest major airport, then driven the remainder of the way through the mountains. But she was worried about her dad.

Abbott Raymond Valentine had turned sixty-nine on his last birthday—which she'd missed because she was at a company retreat in Utah. Her father had been in sort of a funk since his mother had died a few years ago. It didn't feel quite like mourning, but something deeper. She hadn't been able to figure out what it was, and her dad wouldn't open up about what he was feeling. He'd been grumpy and evasive whenever she tried to broach the topic, which ruined the mood of their weekly calls.

So she'd stopped asking, hoping he'd eventually be ready to confide in her.

But two weeks ago, her father had called a big family meeting via teleconference to inform them he needed to see all of them in person. Despite their pleading and threatening, her father wouldn't offer the slightest hint of what this was about. Chandra was terrified about what might prompt her father to gather them together like this for the first time since her grandmother's funeral.

It'd taken three days and an online calendar for the six siblings to figure out when their schedules would permit all of them to take time off their jobs and get together for at least a week, preferably two—as her father had requested. But here she was, on her way to some tiny town in the Smoky Mountains where she only hoped they had internet, cell phone service and indoor plumbing, because hiking in the woods was the limit of her outdoorsyness.

Chandra settled into a seat as far away as she could get from the handsome man with the gorgeous dark eyes who was making her rethink her stance on beards. Because as much as she'd like to get to know him up close and personal, she didn't have time for extracurricular activities on this trip.

She was a problem solver. Had been since she was eight years old and returned from school to discover the *Dear Abbott* letter her mother had left on the kitchen counter.

Her father had been gutted. She, Nolan, Sebastian and Alonzo had been devastated. Just like that, she'd become the adult in the house as her father struggled to deal with her mother's abandonment. In some ways, she'd felt like the only adult in the room with her family ever since.

Chandra rubbed her arms against the chill in the airport, still devastated by the painful memory.

Mr. Handsome stared at her from across the wide expanse.

Chandra pulled the book on teambuilding she'd been reading from her purse and opened it. She couldn't afford to be distracted by the man. She needed to get to the bottom of whatever was going on with her father, solve whatever problem needed to be solved, then return to San Diego.

Julian Brandon returned to his airplane gate clutching a grease-stained bag with a piping hot panini sandwich and fries in one hand and pulling his rolling luggage behind him with the other.

His flight had already boarded.

The woman taking tickets at the door narrowed her gaze and gestured for him to hurry.

"I thought the plane didn't board for another five minutes." He produced his phone so she could scan his boarding pass.

"Everyone was here, so the captain wants to leave as soon as possible. Enjoy your flight."

Julian shoved his phone into his back pocket and made his way through the tunnel. Then he made his way to his seat. At six foot two, being folded into a cramped seat on one of these smaller planes was never a picnic. So while he preferred a window seat, he'd booked an aisle seat so he could stretch his legs. But it appeared he was in luck. The window seat beside him was empty. So he'd have the entire row to himself.

He put his bag in the overhead bin and settled into his seat, prepared to watch an episode or two of a sci-fi show while giving himself a reprieve from thinking about his reluctant return to the little town where he was raised. The town he'd be moving back to for the next four years—and not a day more. Not because he wanted to but because it was part of an obligation he'd made as a fourteen-year-old kid when a local philanthropist offered to sponsor his full ride to college and then med school.

They sealed the door of the plane and the captain announced they would be leaving soon, so everyone should take their seats. Julian breathed a sigh of relief; grateful he'd gotten lucky. He slid over to the window seat.

"Excuse me, but you're sitting in my spot."

Julian looked up and locked eyes with the stunning woman he'd been checking out in the airport terminal. Her black T-shirt said Wake Up, Kick Ass, Repeat in bold white letters. Slim black pants hugged her curves. Her dark brown hair was pushed back with a pricey pair of sunglasses. Her dark brown skin looked flawless and her pursed lips were punctuated with a deep purple lipstick.

Julian sat there, blinking, as if he'd never seen a beautiful woman before.

He was usually much more suave than this. But something about this woman threw him off his game. He was at a loss for words.

"Ma'am, you'll need to take your seat." The flight attendant's bright smile did little to mask her irritation.

"I will." The woman propped a hand on her hip. "As soon as this gentleman gets out of my seat."

"Sorry. Thought I had the row to myself." Julian unbuckled his seat belt and stepped into the aisle, so the woman could get to her seat.

The flight attendant gave him the evil eye, then moved to help an older couple searching for space in the overhead bins.

"Sorry," Julian said to the woman who was buckling her seat belt as she stared out onto the tarmac. "When they shut the door and no one was here, I assumed—"

"That you'd hit the air travel lottery and had the row to yourself?" Her lips twitched with a hint of a smile. She tucked loose strands of hair behind her ear. "Given the situation, I would've made the same assumption. But I was here…just in the restroom." She dropped her gaze, and he wondered if beneath her rich dark brown skin her cheeks were flushed. "When I'm traveling alone, I don't like leaving my things on the seat unattended."

"Understandable." He nodded. After an awkward bit of silence, he extended his hand. "I'm JB, by the way. And I'm not usually a seat stealer."

Her smile broadened. She shook his hand. "Chandra."

"Pleasure to meet you, Chandra." He realized he was smiling like a goober and still holding her hand when she gently tugged it free.

He cleared his throat and focused intently on sticking his phone and tablet into the pocket on the back of the seat in front of him.

Chandra reached into her bag and dug out a pair of premium over-the-ear headphones. A clear sign, if ever he'd seen one, that she had no intention of engaging in conversation.

Message received.

He'd go back to Plan A: catching up on episodes of television shows he never had time to watch. Up until today, he'd been too slammed with residency at a busy hospital in Philadelphia and volunteer work at clinics in both the inner city and rural Pennsylvania to make time for sci-fi escapism…but his life was going to be very different now.

During his going-away party in the hospital cafeteria the night before, his friends had said he should be glad to have a normal schedule and free time. They were jealous that he'd get to have a life now that he was going to be a small-town doctor.

He'd smiled politely and pretended to agree, but truthfully, he knew he'd miss being so busy he barely had time to dwell on his past mistakes—like the fractured relationship with his mother. Now that he was returning to the town where he'd grown up and where his mother still resided, there would be little chance of avoiding those uncomfortable feelings. This plane ride might be his last opportunity *not* to ruminate on what an awful son he was.

As the plane sped along the runway in preparation for their ascent, the woman gripped the armrest between them, her fancy high-heel boots dug into the floor, and she squeezed her eyes shut.

Julian wanted to ask if she was all right. But it would be a stupid question. Clearly, she wasn't. It was also clear Chandra didn't want to be bothered, so he'd respect that.

He just hoped to God this woman wouldn't get sick during the flight.

Before long, they were given the okay to turn on electronics. But the pilot warned that it would likely be a bumpy ride and kept the sign on admonishing them to remain seated with their seat belts fastened.

No air traveler liked turbulence, but it didn't particularly bother him...except when he was trying to watch a show on his tablet and eat his no-longer-hot panini and fries. He stuffed a few of the delicious, lukewarm fries into his mouth, then bit into his sandwich. When he opened his bottle of soda, the woman beside him nearly jumped out of her skin.

Chandra's arms tensed as she white-knuckled her grip on the end of the armrest. She pointed at his iPad screen.

"Is that *Orphan Black*?"

Julian slid one earbud out of his ear and nodded. "Yeah. A couple friends of mine are science fiction geeks. They've been urging me to try the show for years, but they recently gifted me all the seasons. Figured I'd finally give it a try."

"My sister raved about the show when it was on, but I never got around to watching it." Chandra's jaw tightened in response to the dip and sway of the plane. "I'd planned to read, but with all this turbulence, I can't focus."

"Nervous flyer?"

"Not on larger aircraft. Which is why I usually avoid smaller, regional planes." Chandra squeezed her eyes shut momentarily, taking a deep breath before opening them again. "Let's just say I'll be glad when we land."

"You're welcome to watch the show with me," he

suggested, surprising himself. "I'm just starting Episode One. It'll distract you from the bumpy ride and give you something else to focus on."

"I don't want to disturb the other passengers."

"I can share my audio with you." Julian was glad he'd paid attention when his tech geek roommate had shown him this trick. "Just tap the power button on your headset."

She did and he shared his audio with her.

Chandra seemed surprised when the show began playing in her headset. "Thank you, JB."

"My pleasure." He extended the greasy cardboard box toward her. "French fry?"

Chandra stared at them apprehensively, her brows scrunched. Then she thanked him and grabbed two fries. She nibbled thoughtfully while watching the screen where he'd restarted the first episode. Chandra was completely engaged with the show from the opening scene, and he was mesmerized by her.

She was even more beautiful up close. Her sweet, subtle scent reminded him of the honeysuckle that grew along the fence in the backyard of his childhood home. They shared the armrest she'd been clutching for dear life minutes earlier. And the tension in her shoulders seemed to have eased as she focused on the screen of his tablet, propped on his tray.

When he offered her the fries again, she gladly accepted the box. Chandra nibbled quietly on the fries— which she apparently had no plans of relinquishing—as she reacted to each scene. The tense, action-packed show was doing its job—distracting her from the movement of the plane. But as exciting as the show was, he'd rather be spending their time together getting to know her.

There were a dozen questions he wanted to ask: Where was she traveling to? Where was she from? Was this a business or pleasure trip? Would she like to go out for coffee? What would she like for breakfast?

Instead, they watched the screen in silence. Her arm leaned against his, and her warmth seeped into his skin, despite the layers of fabric between them.

Suddenly the turbulence became far more noticeable as the plane dipped and then swayed. The captain requested that everyone take their seats and put away any trays. He complied. And after a particularly violent rumble, Chandra gripped his forearm, her heels pressed into the floor.

Julian placed his hand atop hers and forced a smile, even as his own stomach dipped. "I know it feels scary, Chandra. But everything is going to be fine—I promise."

Chandra jerked her attention toward him, her forehead furrowed by a deep frown. Her mesmerizing eyes were a gorgeous deep shade of chocolate brown, rimmed by a slightly darker hue. Her smoky purple eye shadow made her brown eyes pop, and he honestly couldn't help staring.

Chandra studied him; one perfectly arched brow hiked toward her hairline. She heaved a quiet sigh, and her shoulders slid back into place. She loosened her grip on his forearm but didn't remove her hand. Nor did he remove his hand from hers.

"My brain realizes that, logically, you're in no position to make such a promise. You don't have any control over what the plane does, and for all we know, the pilot and copilot were in the lounge drinking body shots off the flight attendants and smoking J's." She shrugged. "But hearing you promise everything will be fine, like you truly believe it, really does help. So thank you."

Julian's mouth curved in a smile. He had that unsettling feeling in his gut again. Like he was at the top of a roller coaster, counting down the milliseconds until the car would careen down the hill.

What was it about Chandra…he didn't even know her last name…that ignited that kind of reaction?

"Glad I could help." Julian reluctantly removed his hand from atop hers and settled back against his seat.

Chandra released his arm, then frowned when the plane dipped and the cabin rumbled, causing several of the passengers around them to gasp and murmur.

Chandra closed her eyes. "Everything is going to be fine. Everything is going to be fine. Everything is going to be…"

Another bout of rough turbulence hit. Chandra slapped a hand over her mouth, as if to stifle a scream. She was shaking.

"I need you to make good on that promise, JB," she said.

"Did you roller-skate on the sidewalk as a kid?" he asked.

Chandra furrowed her brows. "Sure. Why?"

"Remember how bumpy it was versus skating on a smooth surface, like at the rink? This is like that. Or like driving on a road filled with potholes. It's uncomfortable and creates a bit of drama, but in the end, it's always okay. It will be today, too." Julian winked. "All right?"

Chandra blew out a breath and nodded.

"In the meantime, maybe this will help…"

He switched to a calming Zen playlist he listened to while meditating each morning. It was his way of chilling out despite the stress of medical school and his residency. Since their audio was still linked, the music played through Chandra's headphones, too.

Julian perched his elbow on the armrest between them and opened his palm. "If you get really nervous, you can hold my—"

There was another dip and rumble, and Chandra pressed her palm to his and threaded their fingers. She squeezed tightly, her nails digging into the back of his hand.

Julian squeezed her hand reassuringly, hoping like hell everything would, in fact, be just fine.

Two

Chandra was grateful the plane had finally landed. Her fellow passenger's calm reassurance and the Zen playlist he pumped through her headset had helped her get through the worst bout of turbulence she'd ever experienced.

She released his hand, which she'd been clutching for dear life for the past forty minutes. "I guess I should give that back now." Her cheeks heated with embarrassment. "You'll probably be needing it."

"Once the feeling returns." The man's broad smile as he shook his presumably numb hand put her at ease.

Still, she couldn't help being embarrassed. She'd behaved like a child frightened by a thunderstorm. It was unlike her. She'd always been the one who'd comforted her younger siblings and reassured her father through whatever storms life brought.

And she was the take-charge director of supply chain, logistics and workplace whose claim to fame was her ability to get shit done with an unshakable smile while stepping on the fewest toes possible. She made the hard decisions that needed to be made: budget cuts, department closures, staff reassignments. Whatever it took to keep the company lean and efficient. Even if it meant crying over a bottle of wine that night because she'd been forced to cut someone's job.

When she'd been sent to San Diego with the assignment to "clean house," she'd been dubbed the Smiling Assassin. But she'd established a new company culture and earned the respect of the frontline employees.

Her Achilles' heel, in a position that frequently required travel, was that she didn't much enjoy flying. Thus today's embarrassing display.

She was grateful JB had been seated beside her and that he'd been genuinely sweet, patient and kind. She doubted that coddling a grown woman through a bumpy flight was how he'd planned to spend his day.

"Here's your carry-on." The man's deep, soothing voice stirred her from her daze. He took her black designer bag with hot-pink-and-white flowers printed on it down from the overhead bin and pulled up the handle.

"Thank you again, JB. It was nice meeting you." Chandra extended a hand.

His large, warm hand enveloped hers. He held it for a moment before shaking it.

"The pleasure was definitely *mine*," he said, still holding her hand. His eyes crinkled with a smile, his full, sensuous lips peeking out from beneath his beard.

Her belly did somersaults and her pulse raced.

Chandra tugged her hand from his. Not because she was offended by his flirtation. Because she liked the feel of her hand in his a little too much. For the briefest moment, she'd imagined lifting onto her toes and pressing her mouth to the lush, full lips that taunted her with a sexy little smirk.

"Take care." Chandra lifted the strap of her bag higher on her shoulder.

As she turned to walk away, she could practically feel the heat of his stare warming her skin.

She'd come to town to find out what was going on with her father and to reconnect with her siblings. She hadn't risked her life on a tiny plane to hook up with some ultrahot, lumberjack-looking brother who'd probably developed those muscled biceps and broad shoulders while swinging an axe in the forest.

Still, a tiny part of her was disappointed the handsome man hadn't at least inquired about seeing her again. She would've politely rejected his advance, of course. But it was nice to at least be asked.

Chandra rolled her bag through the tunnel and onto the concourse of the airport in search of strong coffee. Then she headed to the car rental desk so she could make the hour drive to the little town of Magnolia Lake, where she'd been summoned.

According to her GPS app, Chandra was halfway to her destination. She hadn't expected long stretches of lonely country road threaded through wooded areas and vast farms, with not another person in view for miles.

What if she blew a tire or worse?

Stop being so melodramatic.

Everything would be fine. Fretting over worst-case scenarios was just her brain's way of avoiding the issue at hand. Namely, whatever was going on with her father.

Whenever she permitted her mind to wonder about the possibilities, they frightened her. Chandra gripped the steering wheel of the midsize import she'd rented.

"Please be okay, Dad. *Please*." She whispered the words in the emptiness of the car, her heart racing.

No one lived forever; she realized that. Still, she was nearly forty and she would be a daddy's girl until the day she died. Maybe she lived two thousand miles from her father. But across that distance, she still needed to know he was okay and that he would be there whenever she needed him.

Chandra's phone rang. She had been in too much of a hurry to bother syncing it to the rental vehicle. So she reached for the phone, sitting in the cup holder. The name and photo of her youngest sibling, Naya, flashed across the screen.

Nyles and Naya, her father's late-in-life fraternal twins from his second marriage, were the babies of the family and acted the part. Nyles had a different job every time she talked to him. And at nearly twenty-eight, he seemed to be in a perpetual state of finding himself. Meanwhile, Naya had stumbled into being an Instagram influencer. Her little sister made a very comfortable living. She was based in LA, but often took sponsored trips all over the globe. They spoke often and got together once or twice a month.

Chandra had been calling her sister since her plane landed an hour ago. She was in no hurry to respond to Naya now.

She glanced up at the stretch of road in front of her and was startled by the sight of a large black bear and two cubs crossing the road. Chandra dropped her phone and gripped the wheel so tightly that her knuckles ached. She jammed her foot on the brake but didn't floor it. The last thing she wanted was to come to a complete stop with three angry black bears lurking around her.

But as the car hurtled toward the family of bears, the mother bear stood tall and Chandra screamed, swerving the car hard to the right and jamming her foot on the gas this time, hoping she could drive around the bears and get the hell out of there.

Suddenly, the front right wheel of the import spun out on the muddy shoulder. Without traction, the car slid down an embankment.

"No, no, no!" Chandra tried to yank the wheel to the left—back toward the bears who watched her dilemma with mild interest. She tried her best to avoid sliding down the embankment and into a ditch. But the car continued to career off the edge of the road until the vehicle tipped over, tossing her cell phone, purse and lukewarm coffee into the air right before everything came crashing down.

It all happened so fast, she barely had time to think, let alone react. Chandra felt dazed and disoriented. Her wrist and head throbbed, and she was wet and sticky, courtesy of the remnants of her latte. Her chest ached as the seat belt cut into it. Chandra's breathing was labored, and her eyes were still wrenched shut. She didn't dare move. And she hoped to God the bears had continued on their merry way across the road and wouldn't make an awful situation even worse by trying to pry her out of this glorified aluminum can.

After several moments passed without another sound, Chandra pried open one eye, then the other.

Her world had *literally* turned upside down.

Chandra was suspended by the seat belt that cut across her chest uncomfortably as she hung upside down. Blood rushed to her head and her hair hung in her face.

But at least I'm alive... I think.

Her wrist ached, but nothing appeared to be broken or bleeding. Suddenly, the ring of her phone cut through the eerie quietness. She could hear the phone ringing but had no idea where the sound was coming from. And she definitely couldn't reach it.

She tried to unlatch her seat belt, but it was jammed. Both her wrists were sore, and she didn't have the strength to wrench the seat belt loose.

Chandra's eyes flooded with tears and her body ached.

Correction: she wasn't dead *yet*.

Was this the way her story would end?

Three

Julian had opted to take the scenic route to Magnolia Lake. He was driving a vintage tan-and-white 1970 Ford F-100. He'd needed a way to get to town from the airport in Knoxville and his cousin Elias, who owned body shops in Knoxville and Gatlinburg, needed a truck transported to Magnolia Lake. So he was delivering the iconic old truck, which had been completely refurbished.

He hadn't been back home to Magnolia Lake in the last three years. And in the five years preceding that, his visits home had become less and less frequent.

It had been better that way. Each visit home to spend time with his mother had become more painful and awkward than the last. So one year, when his roommate and a few of their friends had invited him to join them in Cancún for Thanksgiving, he'd said yes. His mother had almost sounded relieved when he'd said he wouldn't be home for the holiday.

So when another friend had invited him on a ski trip to Colorado Springs for Christmas, he'd said yes to that, too. Since then, going on some adventure over the holidays had become his tradition. But now, heading back to Magnolia Lake for four years, he could no longer evade the hurt and painful memories each visit home plagued him with.

He could deal with the temporary loss of the things he loved about living in a major East Coast city. Sporting events. Nights out with friends. Being an easy drive from New York and Broadway. What caused an unbearable knot in his gut was being back in the town where his father had died, knowing he was the reason his dad wasn't there. And seeing the resentment in his mother's eyes. Because she, too, blamed him for his father's death.

Julian scratched at his beard, well overdue for a trim.

He'd grown the beard two years ago, at the request of the woman he was seeing. The beard had lasted far longer than the relationship. He'd kept it because it made him look five or ten years older than his thirty years. That put a lot of the older patients he'd seen during his residency at ease. Now that he was returning home to serve as the local GP to people who'd known him since birth, keeping the beard seemed like a good idea. Maybe it would help them take him seriously and realize that he wasn't a kid anymore.

Knowing his mother would hate it gave him a perverse sense of joy.

Julian slowed the old truck when he saw some tire tracks ahead that veered off the road.

What had happened? Was someone hurt?

Julian pulled to the side of the road and turned on the caution lights. Then he hopped out of the truck and went to take a look.

"Shit."

There was a car turned over in the ditch. He'd treated lots of patients who'd been in car accidents. Not all of them had survived—despite his best efforts. He only hoped the occupants of the car had been wearing their seat belts.

Julian slid down the embankment, not caring about the mud soaking his designer jeans and ruining his expensive boots. He approached the car, where a woman hung upside down, unmoving. His stomach knotted.

"Ma'am, are you all right?" He pressed a hand to the window. "Can you hear me?"

She moved the slightest bit, then bobbed her head. "The seat belt is jammed. I can't get out," she mumbled.

He could barely hear her through the glass, but his shoulders sagged with relief at the sound of her voice. She was alive and conscious. He tried opening the door, but it wouldn't budge. "Sit tight. I'm going to get you out of here, all right?"

"I don't expect I'll be going anywhere soon," she said.

Julian couldn't help chuckling, impressed that she didn't seem panicked. And despite needing his help, she was a little bit of a smart-ass. He couldn't help admiring her fight and spirit.

He took a less steep hill to climb back up the embankment and called Elias to request a tow truck. He retrieved his luggage and dug out one of his going-away gifts: a car safety hammer with a built-in seat belt cutter.

Julian shoved his phone into his back pocket and hurried back down the hill, trying hard to ignore the chilly mud that had soaked through his jeans, making them feel five pounds heavier.

"Turn your head and close your eyes," he instructed. "I'm going to break the glass."

When the woman turned her head away and shielded her face with her arms, Julian removed the safety cap from the pointed end of the hammer and looked away as he tapped on the glass. The window shattered, but the safety glass stayed in place. He used the flat hammer-head to knock the glass out of the window, some of the pieces landing in her hair.

"You're doing great. We're almost there." He employed the calm voice he used to put his patients at ease. "Are you injured? Is anything hurting?"

"Just my pride," she muttered. "And my head because the blood is rushing to it."

"Then let's get you down. Brace your hands on my shoulders while I cut you out of this seat belt. I won't let you fall," he promised before she could object.

The woman, who wore a tan jacket, nodded. Her long hair shielded her face. She gripped his shoulders, and he placed a hand on her waist to stabilize her as he sliced through the seat belt.

He held on to her when the seat belt snapped, then eased her out of the car window, legs and bottom first. It was inelegant, but it got the job done and she was out of the car safely.

Julian set her on her feet, a hand on either side of her waist. She wavered slightly and clutched her head.

"Ma'am, are you sure you're all—"

The woman flipped her hair out of her face.

"Chandra?" He was stunned. With the adrenaline rushing through his veins and the scent of coffee splattered throughout the car, Julian hadn't recognized her alluring scent or her voice.

"JB?" Chandra pressed a hand to her forehead, as if she was feeling a bit woozy. She glanced at the cows grazing in the distant pasture. "Am I dreaming?"

"Afraid not. Seems you were in a single-car accident. I was driving along this road and noticed the skid marks veering down the hill, so I stopped to help."

"You're a regular Black Superman, aren't you?" Her voice was filled with more quiet amusement than mockery. "Did you just pop out of a phone booth around here?"

"I prefer to think of myself as Falcon with a dash of Luke Cage." He chuckled, glad she was lucid enough to make jokes.

She cocked her head and studied him for a moment. "Yeah, I guess I can see that. Now, I need to find my phone." When she turned toward the car, she swayed. He reached out to steady her.

"Are you sure you're okay? Maybe I should call an ambulance. You might've sustained a concussion or—"

"I'm fine." She pressed a hand to her forehead. "I didn't hit my head. I'm just not sure how long I was hanging upside down." Chandra ran her fingers through her hair, which was still a little wild. Pieces of glass fell from it. "I just need to get my things and call my family."

"My cousin owns a couple body shops. He's got a guy in the area. The tow truck should be here any minute." Julian placed a hand on her arm, hoping to calm her. She seemed panicked about not being able to locate her phone. "But if you need to call your family, you can use my phone."

"Thanks. I—" Chandra frowned midsentence. "I...I don't remember any of their numbers."

"Are you experiencing any nausea, double vision or ringing in your ears?" Julian pulled out his phone, his heart rate accelerating. "If so, I'm calling an ambulance right now."

"I don't remember their numbers because I *never* dial them. They're saved in my cell phone." Chandra placed a hand over his to prevent him from making the call. "*Please* don't make a fuss—this is embarrassing enough."

"What happened exactly?"

Chandra's eyes widened and she glanced around at the open fields. "Did you see that mother bear and her two cubs?"

"I didn't." He still wasn't convinced she wasn't suffering from a head injury.

"They were there—I assure you. My phone rang and I glanced down to see who it was. When I looked up again, there were *freaking bears* crossing the road. I tried to go around them, but I lost traction on the shoulder and ended upside down in this ditch." Chandra folded her arms. "Those damn bears owe me a rental car."

"Yeah? Well, good luck with getting them to pay up." Julian was dirty, tired and hungry. He needed a steaming shower, a hot meal and a warm bed. Yet he couldn't help being amused by this woman who was gorgeous, even if she was a little worse for wear after her tumble down the hill. "I'll help you up to the road. We can wait in the truck until the tow truck arrives. Once your rental car is out of the ditch, we'll retrieve your things."

"I'm sorry if I'm grouchy right now. I just can't believe this happened. I'm usually so careful when I drive."

"The important thing is you're all right." Julian held his hand out to her. "Come on. The hill is less steep up there. It'll be easier for you to climb up it in those boots." He regarded her feet, clad in a pair of sexy black leather boots that had done things to him the moment he'd seen her prancing through the airport in them.

Chandra took his hand and they climbed back up the hill. She stomped the mud from her boots, and he helped her inside the truck, thankful his cousin had been overly cautious and had covered the floor and seats in several layers of heavy plastic.

But his clothing was soaked through with mud. He doubted the plastic would be enough to protect the newly recovered leather seats.

"This is a customer's truck. I'm transporting it for my cousin, so I can't get it all muddy," Julian said. "I'm going to grab my luggage and change into some dry clothes."

"Of course." Chandra raked her fingers through her damp hair and fanned her shirt, stained with coffee. "I promise not to look." One corner of her mouth curved in a sexy smirk.

It was the most Chandra had flirted with him since they'd met, but he tried not to read too much into it. He cleaned his hands on a rag, then dug into his bag for clean T-shirts and sweats.

He opened the truck door and handed her a long-sleeve gray shirt bearing a blue bison and the name of his alma mater—Howard University—in bold red. "In case you'd like to get out of that sticky shirt. I won't look either. Promise."

"Thanks, JB."

Julian stripped down to his boxers and kicked off his muddy shoes and socks. He dropped the wet, dirty clothing and shoes in a plastic bag. Then he tugged a long-sleeve navy blue Howard T-shirt over his head. He pulled on gray sweats, then slipped on his Adidas running shoes.

"You good?" he called before approaching the driver's side.

"All changed," Chandra replied.

Julian climbed into the driver's seat and couldn't help smiling. She looked great in his old college T-shirt, despite it being too big for her.

Chandra shoved the sleeves up. "Much better. Thanks."

"And you're sure you're—"

"I'm fine. *Really*," Chandra insisted. "Like I said, my pride is more hurt than anything else."

"Could've happened to anyone." He nodded toward the rearview mirror. "Here comes the tow truck driver now."

Julian turned the idling truck off and they both hopped out. Once the rental car was out of the ditch, they retrieved her belongings. She called the rental company and they arranged for the tow driver to return the car to Knoxville.

"I know you're probably tired and your family is expecting you," Julian said while Chandra was on hold with the rental company. "I'd be happy to drop you wherever you need to go. You can arrange to have them deliver a car to you later."

Chandra frowned, her adorable nose scrunching. "You've already done so much for me. I don't want to impose any further."

"I'm headed to Magnolia Lake, about half an hour up the road. How far do you need to go?" he asked.

"I'm headed there, too. To this address." She held up her phone.

"I know the area. It's on the way into town." Julian rubbed his beard. "There are mostly farms and ranches out there, on the outskirts. It's on the way."

Chandra's dark brown eyes flickered with amusement. "I don't mean to sound ungrateful, but haven't I caused you enough trouble for one day?"

"Maybe I needed a little adventure." Julian shrugged, his hands shoved into the pockets of his gray sweats.

Chandra gave him a reluctant smile. But when the operator returned, she made arrangements for a car to be delivered to her in Magnolia Lake.

Julian grinned. He hadn't asked Chandra for her number when they'd parted on the plane. But fate had given him another chance. This time, he'd definitely shoot his shot.

Four

There was something inherently calming about JB. He'd settled her nerves on the plane and reassured her as he'd rescued her from her vehicle.

The warm tenor of his deep voice had sluiced over her skin like warm honey while he'd graciously made her feel less bad about wrecking her rental car on an open country road.

As they drove past a sign welcoming them to Magnolia Lake, home of the King's Finest Distillery, JB had asked whom she was visiting. Chandra had reluctantly explained.

"I keep thinking of all the possible reasons my father would call us out to a tiny town in the middle of nowhere. None of them are good." Chandra rubbed her arms as she scanned the road in search of more migratory bears.

Julian cranked up the heat. "I can understand why you'd be worried. But let's hope your dad has a positive reason for bringing you all here. Like maybe he's planning to move to Magnolia Lake."

"Why would he move here? Not that Magnolia Lake isn't a perfectly lovely place to live," she added quickly.

"It is," he said, only slightly defensive.

"Yet you couldn't wait to escape and haven't been back in three years?" Chandra's smile widened when JB's did.

"The urge to put as much mileage as you can between yourself and the small town you grew up in is a rite of passage for two-thirds of the kids who grow up in them," he said with a slight chuckle. "But in the end, a lot of folks develop appreciation for home and return."

"Like you?" she asked.

On the plane, JB had mentioned that he was returning home after being away for several years. He hadn't seemed thrilled about it. Chandra was curious as to why he'd chosen to return, but it seemed like an intrusive question to ask a complete stranger. She hoped her current prompt would elicit more details.

"My dad died in a traffic accident when I was a kid. Being home reminds me of that." Deep lines spanned his forehead as his brows furrowed. "Probably not the healthiest approach, but I've avoided returning home as much as possible."

"I'm sorry. I didn't realize—"

"Not a big deal." He stared ahead as they hugged a curve in the road. "Besides, it was a long time ago."

"When it comes to losing a parent, it always feels like it happened yesterday." Chandra sighed.

"How'd you lose your mom?" He glanced at her momentarily.

"She walked out when I was eight." Chandra shrugged. "Raising four kids under the age of ten while her husband worked sixty-plus-hour weeks in the family business apparently wasn't her thing. Haven't seen her since."

It'd been thirty-one years since Mary Valentine had walked away. Yet a hole practically burned through her chest every time Chandra talked about it.

"I'm sorry, Chandra." JB squeezed the hand that gripped the edge of the seat. "I lost my dad when I was ten. But something about being back here... It feels like it happened yesterday."

The heat from JB's large hand enveloped hers. Warmth trailed up her arm, her skin tingling in its wake. When she'd held his hand on the plane, she'd been so nervous about the flight that she hadn't been able to take in anything else. She'd been simply clinging to him like a lifeline. But now she was distinctly aware of the strength of his hand, the warmth of his skin pressed against hers. And she was reminded of how attracted she'd been to JB the moment she'd laid eyes on him in that airport. A distraction she couldn't afford.

Chandra discreetly tugged her hand from his. She raked her fingers through her hair. She could only imagine what a mess she must be. Thankfully, JB had been kind enough not to mention it.

"My family has owned a very successful textile firm in Nashville for several generations. My father has been devoted to the place his entire life. In fact, his dedication to work was a point of contention between him and my mom," Chandra explained. "We have a sizable family estate in Nashville. So why would he suddenly want to own property here?"

"Lots of people own cabins around here for fishing and hunting or just to get away from the hustle and bustle of city life."

Her father and brothers did like to fish. But even if her dad had purchased a cabin here, what about that would be so urgent that he'd insist they all needed to come see it?

"I don't know. It just doesn't make sense." Chandra rubbed the chill bumps that suddenly formed on her arms, despite the heat pumping in the truck.

"Guess you won't have to wait long to find out." JB nodded toward a sign that said Richardson Vineyards. "We're here."

"Are you sure this is the address I gave you?" She studied the sign and the vast property surrounding it.

He read off the address and she checked it against the one in her dad's text message. The address was the same, but maybe it was a typo. Why would her father want them all to converge on a broken-down old winery? "This has to be a mistake."

Another car whipped into the driveway and pulled around them. It was a black convertible with the top down, despite the chilly fall weather. A song by Doja Cat blared from the speakers and her baby sister was behind the wheel wearing a dark pair of designer shades. Likely a gift from one of her high-end sponsors. A hot-pink wig shaped in an adorable bob framed Naya's gorgeous face.

She whipped into a space in the small paved lot near cars Chandra recognized as her father's and younger brothers'.

"I guess it is the right place. That's my sister." Chandra studied the large old house sorely in need of a paint job, a new roof and several other repairs. She stepped down from the truck carefully. There were more potholes than pavement in the parking lot. "Sorry in advance for anything uncouth my baby sister is about to say."

"Duly noted." JB chuckled as he stepped out of the truck. "I'll grab your bags from the back."

"Hey, sis." Naya waved as she slid her sunglasses atop her head. "I was on the phone with Erica when you called the first few times. I tried to call you back, but I can see you've been...*busy*." Naya lifted her eyebrows mischievously as she studied JB letting down the tailgate and bending over to reach for Chandra's luggage.

It was the first time she'd seen JB from behind. And to be fair, the man was in possession of an incredibly impressive set of glutes, spotlighted by ass-hugging gray sweats.

Chandra's cheeks heated and there was a fluttering low in her belly. A man with a traffic-stopping ass was *definitely* her weakness. Not that she'd dated much in the five years since her engagement had ended.

"You're blushing," Naya whispered loudly as she poked her in the side and giggled.

"First of all, you couldn't tell if I was blushing." Chandra held up a finger, thankful for her deep brown skin. "Second, did no one ever teach you how to whisper? Because the point of it is to *not* be overheard by other people."

JB snorted, glancing away when they turned toward him.

"See what I mean?" Chandra gestured toward JB.

"Hi, I'm Naya Valentine." Her sister extended a hand and batted the ultralong mink eyelashes nature definitely hadn't gifted her with. She nodded her head toward Chandra. "I'm this one's baby sister. And you are?"

"This is JB," Chandra said quickly. "We met on the plane. The rest I'll tell you later."

She'd opted not to call her family once she'd finally located her phone. Her car was being taken care of, and she already had a ride to the house. There was no point in alarming them for nothing. Thanks to JB, she was fine.

"I'll see you inside in a few. But in the meantime, could you pop your trunk? That way, JB can put my bags inside until we figure out where we'll be staying. Assuming there's room in there."

Her sister traveled heavy. She usually had a full suitcase just for her makeup and colorful wigs.

Naya popped the trunk, as requested.

"I'm surprised Erica didn't come with you," Chandra said.

Naya frowned at the mention of her current love interest. The two had been together a little more than a year. They'd met at an Instagram influencer convention.

"We'll talk about that later, too." There was a hint of sadness in Naya's dark brown eyes, though she turned up the wattage on her ever-present smile. "Nice to meet you, JB. I hope we'll be seeing you again soon."

Chandra turned to the handsome man whose warm gaze made her temperature rise and her stomach do flips. "Thanks for everything, JB. I don't know what I would've done without you today."

"You would've managed fine. I have no doubt of that." He scratched at his beard and flashed a devilish smile that sent heat rocketing up her spine and left her wondering about the taste of his full lips.

She shuddered, ignoring the beading of her nipples and the steady pulse between her thighs.

"Well, I'm really glad I didn't have to find out."

"Let me put these bags in your sister's trunk." He grabbed her bags and moved toward the open deck lid of her sister's rented convertible. She walked over with him, impressed when he managed to squeeze her two bags inside the space overflowing with her sister's Gucci luggage, stamped with the company's iconic logo.

When Chandra closed the trunk, she winced in pain.

"You *did* hurt yourself." JB's eyebrows furrowed with concern as he examined her wrist. An angry bruise had become visible and her wrist was much sorer than it'd been before. "That's a nasty bruise, Chandra. Can you move your wrist?"

"Yes, it's… *Ow*," she muttered as the pain shot up her arm when she tried to move her wrist in a circle. "It's fine. Just a little sore."

"You have complete range of motion, but still, it could be a bad sprain. If the pain persists or if that headache doesn't go away—"

"The headache is already gone, and my wrist is fine. But I promise to see someone about it if it's still hurting in a couple of days," she said.

"All right, then." JB let go of her hand and she couldn't help feeling a bit disappointed.

You are not here to hook up with the sweet, sexy lumberjack with the perfect ass. You're here to see about Dad.

"Well, thanks again." Chandra hugged JB, trying to ignore how wonderful it felt as he wrapped her in his solid arms and squeezed her to his chest. She reluctantly pulled free of his embrace. "It was really nice meeting you, JB."

She shoved the too-long sleeve back up her arm—then remembered where she'd gotten it. "Your shirt. I'll run inside and change so I can give it back to you."

"How long will you be in town?" JB asked.

"A week, maybe two." She shrugged.

"I'll get it next time we see each other." A flirtatious grin curved one side of his sexy mouth.

Electricity crackled down her spine. She folded her arms over her chest and tried to ignore her body's reaction to the possibility of them seeing each other again.

"I have no idea what I'm walking into here. So it doesn't feel right making plans."

"Fair." He nodded sagely, folding his arms and widening his stance. "But I'm betting your dad invited you here for a happy reason. If I'm right, you call me and then we can meet for coffee maybe. You can bring the shirt then." His dark eyes glinted in the sunlight. "Deal?"

She pushed her hair, still sticky with coffee, behind her ear and nodded. "Sure. Why not?"

He grinned. "Pen?" He nodded toward her purse.

Chandra produced a pen from her handbag and JB scribbled his name and a phone number on the white plastic bag she'd put her coffee-stained shirt in. He returned the pen and headed toward the truck.

"Hey, what if…? I mean…what if I can't go out with you?"

"Then you can keep it." JB winked, then hopped into the truck and drove off.

Chandra watched him drive off, wishing they'd met under different circumstances. Then she turned and surveyed the old house more closely.

With its deep gold stucco, terra-cotta roof and antique arched double doors, it looked like a Tuscan villa that had been transported to the Smoky Mountains from another place and time.

Rather than the typical front porch she was accustomed to seeing on Southern homes, the house had a bona fide loggia. The Italian-style porch ran the length of the front of the house. Its stucco-covered columns formed arches that ran across the entire structure. Black wrought iron lanterns and sconces—in desperate need of refinishing or replacement—dotted the walls and hung from the ceiling.

The stucco exterior was stained and discolored. In some places, there were substantial cracks. Still, the place had enormous potential. If the owners would put some money into it, the building would make a great space for wine tastings and small events. Maybe even small wedding receptions. But in its current state, it felt as if she was risking her life just climbing the three cracked stucco stairs.

Chandra pushed open the heavy antique wooden door her sister had disappeared through earlier. She stepped inside and scanned the dark, dated decor. A beautiful young woman stood behind the large front desk made of dark wood. Behind her, the words *Richardson Vineyards* were burned into a wooden wall.

"Welcome, Ms. Valentine." The woman offered a

guarded smile that revealed none of her teeth and didn't reach her eyes. "I'm Dejah Richardson, the vineyard manager. Your family is waiting for you in the game room. If you'll follow me."

Chandra followed the woman through a large, sunny great room with dated decor and a few gorgeous antiques. They walked down a long narrow hall past the dining room with a large table. Finally, Dejah opened another antique door and Chandra heard the voices of her siblings.

Chandra stepped inside. "Hello, everyone."

The space went quiet.

Her brothers—Nolan, Sebastian, Alonzo and Nyles—had tentative expressions that matched her own. Her sister, Naya, had been chatting happily with their father, who appeared to be in an equally cheerful mood.

Given the gravity with which he'd impelled their presence here and his generally bleak mood for the past few years, Chandra was surprised to see her father so upbeat.

Maybe JB was right. Perhaps her father had summoned them all to this place for a happy reason. The family equivalent of a company retreat, perhaps? After all, they'd grown apart over the past five years or so. And she was likely to blame for that.

After her mother's unexpected departure, Chandra had made it her mission to be the single thread holding their family together. But following her failed engagement, she'd needed a change.

A part of her had grown resentful that she was still the one always cleaning up the family messes. So she'd done something unexpected. She'd left their family's textile firm and taken a job in San Diego with Phillips Athletic Wear.

Her father had been hurt but understood that she needed some space. Naya, who had an inherent gift for rolling with the punches, easily adapted. Her four brothers had been decidedly less understanding.

Nolan, the CFO of Valentine Textiles, a company started by her paternal great-grandfather and run by her father, had said it felt like she'd pulled the rug out from under them.

Maybe she had. But it had forced all of her siblings to become less dependent on her. Alonzo, Nyles and Naya—the three youngest—were forced to finally grow up, handle their business and clean up their own messes.

Chandra had spent the past five years consumed with her work. Her relationships with Nolan, Sebastian and Alonzo had become distant. And without her there to coordinate family vacations, holidays and general family get-togethers, they'd become like individual satellites circling their father but rarely connecting.

She felt bad about that. So maybe a family retreat was *exactly* what they needed.

"Glad you could make it." Nolan hugged her.

Chandra hugged Nolan back, ignoring the hidden jab referencing all the times she hadn't been able to make it home for birthdays, company celebrations and a few major holidays. "Good to see you, Nole."

Nolan adjusted his ever-smudged glasses, his smile shifting to a more genuine one. "You too, Chandra."

She exchanged similar greetings with Sebastian, Valentine Textiles' VP of operations, and Alonzo, who worked for an advertising firm in New York.

Nyles, whom she still spoke to regularly, gave her a warm hug. "Good to see you, sis."

"Now that your hot new *friend* is gone, maybe I can finally get a hug." Naya approached her with a mock pout.

"You brought some dude to the family meeting?" Alonzo raised one of his thick brows and frowned.

"No, I didn't." Chandra gave Naya the evil eye, then hugged her little sister, getting a whiff of her delicate perfume. Chandra released Naya and pointed a finger at her. *"Snitch."*

"Guess some things never change." Alonzo chuckled. Naya gave his arm a playful punch.

"That perfume smells amazing and insanely expensive," Chandra noted.

"It is." Naya smiled proudly. "A gift from my latest sponsor. I'm doing a photo shoot in France with them in February."

"Good for you." Chandra squeezed her sister's arm.

They'd all been a little worried when Naya had graduated college, spent two years traveling the world, then declared that she was going to become a full-time Instagram influencer rather than joining the family textile firm. But in the past four years she'd continued to increase both her income and her follower count while working on her own terms.

Chandra envied her little sister for that.

"Guess I'll just stand over here and be ignored." Her father folded his arms and tried to look serious, but a slow grin spread across his handsome face.

"I always save the best for last." Chandra smiled.

"Am I the only one who feels insulted by that?" Sebastian's dark eyes flickered.

"Hush, Bas." Chandra crossed the room and hugged her father. She settled into her dad's lingering embrace and inhaled his familiar scent. Abbott Raymond Valentine gave the best hugs. They made everything better. "Missed you, Dad."

"Missed you too, pumpkin." He hadn't called her that in years.

A knot tightened in Chandra's stomach. She searched her father's dark eyes. "What's going on, Dad?"

"Have a seat, and I'll tell you everything. Promise."

Chandra sank onto the love seat beside Naya. Tension rolled off her sister's slim shoulders and marred the handsome faces of her four brothers.

Clearly, she wasn't the only one worried about their dad.

Five

Ray Valentine adjusted his glasses as he surveyed the faces of his children. They were worried by this cryptic meeting he'd called, and they'd probably think he was losing it once he shared his big news. A valid concern, given that his own mother had battled dementia the last several years of her life. Still, he hoped they'd see things his way in the end.

"Thank you all for coming. I know it wasn't easy to re-arrange your schedules on such short notice. But I thought it best if I told you all this in person and all at once."

"Told us *what*, Dad?" Chandra gripped her younger sister's hand as the two of them huddled together on the love seat. "Are you not feeling well?"

"I'm fine, sweetheart." He felt guilty about the pained look on his eldest daughter's face.

She wore her heart on her sleeve and believed it her

job to take care of everyone in her life. She'd taken the abandonment by her mother, then stepmother, particularly hard. And when her fiancé had suddenly called off their wedding, it had been more than his sweet girl could take.

When Chandra had pulled away, he hadn't tried to stop her. After she'd practically raised her siblings, he couldn't blame her for finally putting her needs first.

"A few months before your gram passed, she said to me, 'I love you, son. You've always been such a good boy. But you're just not...*him*.'"

"You're just not *whom*?" Sebastian furrowed his brows.

"She probably didn't realize who you were. It's the nature of the disease." Nyles shifted to the edge of his seat.

"She knew *exactly* who I was." Ray sank onto the broken-in leather chair. "It was the most lucid she'd been in years."

"Then what do you think she meant?" Alonzo rubbed his chin.

"I didn't know, but it felt important, like something that could explain the disconnect I've always felt between us." He glided a hand over his thinning hair. "After she passed, I was going through her papers and found my real birth certificate and the birth and death certificates for a son I never knew my parents had."

"You had a brother?" Sebastian asked. "What happened to him?"

"His name was Charles, and he drowned in the pond on the family estate when he was three—five years before I was born."

"And neither of your parents ever mentioned him?" Alonzo was on the edge of his seat now, too. "There were no photos in the family albums…nothing?"

"There were two photo albums in her safe-deposit box along with the vital certificates and a few other items," he confirmed. "Those two there."

Ray nodded toward the albums he'd left on the table.

"That's…wild." Sebastian picked up one of the albums and thumbed through it so his brothers could see its contents.

Naya picked up the other and flipped through it as Chandra looked on.

"So when Nana said, 'You're just not him,' she was referring to Charles. The child she lost before you were born." Chandra's eyes filled with tears.

"Correct."

"That's messed up." Nyles handed the album to Alonzo. "Gram was comparing you to a brother you didn't even know you had."

"No." The word caught in Ray's throat. "She was comparing me to their son."

His children, except Nolan, exchanged confused glances.

"But if Charles was their son, that would make him your brother." Sebastian cocked his head. "Unless…"

"What did you mean when you said you found your *real* birth certificate?" Chandra stood. "Are you saying—"

"Eugene and Melba Valentine were not my biological parents. They adopted me when I was two months old, after my mother died."

Chandra moved behind his chair and leaned down to wrap her arms around his neck. "I'm so sorry, Daddy."

"It's okay, baby girl." He patted her arm. "Part of me was relieved to learn the truth. After that, it all finally made sense."

"What made sense?" Nyles asked.

"Why I felt like a disappointment to her. Why it seemed as if looking at me brought her pain. It did—but not because of anything I'd done wrong. I just reminded her of the child she'd lost."

Ray shifted in his seat, making room for Chandra to perch on the edge, her head against his shoulder.

"After I discovered the birth certificates, I went to my mother's sister—your great-aunt Imogene. When I told her I knew the truth, she filled in the missing pieces. My mother didn't want to adopt. She wanted to keep trying to have a child of their own. But my father was an only child and had a heart condition. He was afraid they wouldn't have an heir to leave the company to. And he wanted the textile company to stay in the family and be run the way he'd run it."

"You were their replacement kid." Naya's voice ached with sadness.

"Yes." The truth of that statement hit him in the chest with the weight of a two-ton wrecking ball. "Which explains why my father was so desperate to teach me all there was to know about Valentine Textiles. He started taking me to the office when I was five. He wasn't unkind, mind you, but he was laser focused on me learning the family business inside out."

"*Their* family business." Nyles frowned.

"*Our* family business. They're still my parents. They raised me the best they knew how and gave me a good life," Ray said. It was a line he'd repeated to himself whenever the anger started to build in his chest, like a volcano threatening to explode. "But my father was too focused on the legacy of his company to realize I needed him to be my dad first. And my mother was struggling with the death of her child and the guilt she felt over it. Maybe that's why she seemed incapable of bonding with me. She was never harsh, but she was distant." He shrugged. "Maybe she was afraid to get too close to another child she could lose."

Chandra squeezed his hand, her touch filled with warmth and comfort. She had always managed to bring him a sense of peace when he was at his lowest.

"That's no excuse for how they treated you." Naya's big brown eyes filled with unshed tears.

"Maybe. But I don't want you to think ill of your grandparents. That isn't why I invited you here."

"Why *are* we here?" Sebastian frowned more than any of his children. He wished his son would learn to relax.

"And don't you want to know about your biological family?" Alonzo asked.

"Yes." Ray nodded. "I spent the past couple of years trying to locate them. My birth certificate revealed the identity of my mother, but the line for my father's name had been left blank. Now I know why. He died a few hours after my birth on a road between the hospital where I was born and his house. I believe he came to the hospital to see me or maybe he was there for the birth. I don't know." Ray shrugged. "But he didn't make it back home to his family."

"He was married?" Chandra asked.

"Yes."

"So who was this philandering grandfather of ours?" Alonzo topped off his glass with the bottle of King's Finest Bourbon on the table in front of him.

Ray indicated the glass in his son's hand. "King Abbott."

Alonzo froze, the glass perched inches from his lips. "As in *the* King Abbott? The founder of the distillery?"

"King didn't start the distillery. He was a bootlegger who ran moonshine in the hollers in these mountains. It was his son Joseph who founded King's Finest as a legitimate distillery long after his father's death."

"Joseph Abbott is your half brother?" Chandra's eyes widened. "Is that why we're here? You're planning to… what? Confront him with this?"

"That's *part* of the reason you're here," Ray clarified. "But there won't be any messy confrontations. I met Joe and his family a couple weeks ago, when they opened that new restaurant of theirs. He was as stunned as I was to learn the news. It took a DNA test to convince him, and it's something we're both still trying to wrap our heads around. But we've chatted quite a bit since then."

The room was dead silent as each of his children absorbed this new information.

"Does that mean we get free liquor?" Nyles asked. "Because their top-shelf bourbon is *banging*. I could definitely use a case of that."

"What the hell is wrong with you?" Sebastian asked. "You are *not* going to embarrass us by asking for free liquor."

"Relax, dude. I was kidding." Nyles poured bourbon into his glass, looking like a puppy that had just gotten scolded for whizzing on the carpet.

"We're doing just fine. We certainly don't need any handouts." Ray gave his youngest son a pointed look. That boy was going to be the death of him. He was sure of it. "But I would like you all to meet your uncle and cousins. They're not just successful. They're good people. And despite the awkwardness of the situation, they're eager to meet you all. They're throwing a party for the entire town this weekend and we're the guests of honor."

"Joseph Abbott is throwing a party to introduce the entire town to his long-lost illegitimate brother and his six brats?" Sebastian cranked up an eyebrow. "I find it hard to believe he'd want to publicize his family's dirty laundry."

Ray cringed at Sebastian's reference to him as the Abbott family's "dirty laundry." But he understood what his son was getting at.

"It doesn't feel like something that would benefit their company image," Chandra agreed.

"That brings me to the other reason you're all here." Ray stood, retrieving his bourbon and soda from the table.

He walked to the window and regarded the rows of grapevines, already preparing themselves for the next harvest. Then he turned back toward the six faces staring at him expectantly.

"Discovering that King Abbott was my biological father gave me a renewed sense of purpose. I needed to learn *everything* I could about him. I hired an award-winning genealogist who was able to discover a lot, including that he'd experimented with wine-making."

"It must've stunned you to learn you two have that in common," Chandra said.

Wine-making was a hobby he and his oldest son, Nolan, shared. They worked in an old greenhouse on their family estate in Nashville and had gotten good at making small batches of wine.

"I was. King ran moonshine because there was good money in it, but he had a passion for making wine. He'd hoped to branch out into wine-making professionally. I believe that's how he met my mother. Her family owned a small vineyard. *This* one." Ray held up his palms and glanced around the space.

"We're related to the Richardsons, too?" Nyles seemed panicked by this. Undoubtedly because he'd been flirting shamelessly with Dejah Richardson since he'd arrived.

"Dejah isn't a relative—relax, son." Ray chuckled and so did Nolan and Alonzo. "The property has been sold three times since my biological mother's death. First to an Italian family who bought a neighboring property and built this incredible house and the outlying villas. They even had much of the material imported from Italy. When the family decided to move back to Italy, they sold the property to the Richardsons, who expanded the vineyard to its current size. They produced a phenomenal product, but they weren't the best businesspeople." He lowered his voice. "And, as you can see, they haven't invested much money into keeping up the place."

"So we're here to meet the Abbotts and to connect with our grandmother's history?" Alonzo set his glass down.

"Wait… You said that the property has been sold

three times since your mother's death." Sebastian held up three fingers. "Who owns the property now?"

"We're the new owners."

"What?" five of his children said simultaneously. There was a brief moment of silence followed by the chaos of everyone speaking at once.

"Dad, please tell me you didn't impulse buy this vineyard," Chandra pleaded.

"When you say *we* own it...who exactly do you mean by *we*?" Alonzo frowned.

"How could you make a decision like this without consulting any of us?" Sebastian demanded.

"I don't know that none of us were consulted." Naya folded her arms and nodded toward Nolan. "Because Dad's wine-making buddy over there is suspiciously quiet, and he doesn't seem nearly as shocked by this revelation as the rest of us."

Every head in the room swiveled toward Nolan. His oldest son adjusted his smudged glasses and shifted in his seat. He shrugged. "I'm the CFO of Valentine Textiles."

"What has that got to do with Dad purchasing this place?" Chandra cocked her head. Then everyone's attention shifted back to Ray.

He downed the rest of his bourbon and soda and set his glass down. He stood tall, tipped his chin and spoke with conviction. "Because I'm selling Valentine Textiles."

He ignored the audible gasps in the room and continued.

"We received an offer from a California conglomerate that's been trying to buy the place for years. I was going to turn them down again, but then I realized that I've always resented the firm. It's never been my passion. My parents *acquired* me for the purpose of taking over the business. That's why it's always felt like an albatross around my neck. I don't want any part of it anymore. I want to build something *I'm* passionate about. Create my own legacy…like Joseph has."

"Dad, I understand how you must feel." Chandra's eyes were filled with concern. "But buying this old vineyard on a nostalgic whim with the hopes of turning it into something comparable to what the Abbotts have built… Dad, that's unreasonable. It's taken them fifty-plus years and three generations to build their empire."

"That's why I said *we* own this place." He gestured around the room with a soft smile. "I want this to be *our* legacy. Something we can build *together*. Something we can all be truly passionate about."

Sebastian stood, his eyes filled with hurt and anger. "So just like that, you're selling the textile firm? Without consulting anyone except Nole?" Sebastian gestured toward his brother. "You made this decision with *zero* consideration for the fact that I've dedicated my *entire* career to running and growing the firm. Maybe that doesn't matter to Nolan. But did you even, for a second, consider how that would make me feel?"

Except for the twins, all of his children had worked for Valentine Textiles—though Alonzo and Chandra had eventually ventured elsewhere. But Nolan and Sebastian had spent their entire careers with the family firm, serving as the CFO and VP of operations, respectively. He regretted that they'd followed his example and made Valentine Textiles their lives. And like him, they both had brief, failed marriages because of it.

Ray drew in a pained breath. He'd known that Sebastian would be most upset by his sale of the firm. But he couldn't regret *finally* making a choice that felt right for him. He just wished Sebastian hadn't been hurt by his decision.

"Of course I did, son. And I'm sorry to disappoint you. I appreciate everything you and your brother have done to increase the value of Valentine Textiles. That's why I insisted that you and Nolan be kept on by the new owners, if you choose to stay. I've already talked to Nolan about it. He's all in with building this new business. But there will always be a place at the textile firm for you, if you want it. They'd be thrilled to keep a Valentine as the face of the company. Even asked if I thought you'd make a good fit for the role of CEO."

Sebastian seemed stunned. "You recommended me as CEO?"

"Why not? You're passionate. Knowledgeable. Qualified. And you're ready, if that's what you really want." Ray placed a hand on his son's shoulder. "But I'd prefer to have you here with me. Building our own legacy on land once owned by my mother's people. Doing the work my father once hoped to do. Not because I feel obligated to, but because it's my passion, too. I've never felt as at peace or at home as I've felt since the day I walked onto this property."

"Dad, I appreciate why you bought this place. I can even understand why you'd take the deal to sell the firm. But we all have lives of our own," Chandra said. "I'm in San Diego. Naya is in LA. Alonzo is in New

York. Nyles is in Atlanta. You don't honestly expect us to drop the careers we've been building because you've suddenly decided to try your hand at creating an empire as a vintner," Chandra continued. "This dream of yours…what if you change your mind in a few months? Or what if it just doesn't work?"

"The textile company might not be exciting, but the market is steady and so is the income it produces," Alonzo added. "What you're asking, Dad…we'd be taking one hell of a risk."

Alonzo wasn't wrong. Each of his children owned stock in the textile firm. Shares gifted to them at birth and then on their twenty-first birthdays. Shares that helped fund their current lifestyles. Nyles, in particular. Asking them to leave their high-paying careers and lose their quarterly stock payouts was a huge gamble. But he had a plan to make it worth the risk.

"I'm not asking any of you to step out on a wing and a prayer. If you decide to join Valentine Vineyards—" his soul surged just saying the words aloud to his children for the first time "—it will be in a generously paid role—comparable to your current salaries."

Now I've got their attention.

"And if you'll give me three years here at the vineyard, helping me turn this into the empire I believe it can be, you'll receive one-seventh of the sale price of the textile firm *plus* the interest that will have accrued during that time."

"It's a generous offer, Dad," Chandra said after a few minutes. "But this is a lot to take in. Mind if we take some time to think about it?"

Ray hadn't expected this to come easily. And he still

expected a fight from Sebastian and Alonzo. They'd probably try to convince their siblings that he needed a conservatorship.

"Fair enough, sweetheart." He gripped Chandra's left hand and was startled when she yelped. "What's wrong, honey?"

"I had a run-in with a bear and got into an accident on my way into town." Chandra cradled her wrist.

The room was in commotion as everyone inquired about what had happened. Ray wrapped ice in a cloth napkin and placed it on Chandra's wrist as she told them about the man she'd met on the plane who'd apparently saved his daughter's life.

"So this dude steals your seat on the plane, comes off all knight in shining armor during your flight, then just happens to be the guy who comes to your rescue when your car ends up in a ditch?" Sebastian rubbed his chin suspiciously and shook his head. "That's too much of a coincidence. I don't like it."

"Which part is it exactly that you don't like, Sebastian?" Chandra narrowed her gaze at her always cynical brother. "The part where JB kept me from having a panic attack on the plane or the part where he saved me from dying alone in a ditch?"

Nyles chuckled and put a hand on Sebastian's shoulder. "Trust me, bro. You're not gonna win this one. I suggest you let it go."

"And I suggest you be grateful to this JB." Naya folded her arms. "Otherwise, we'd be sitting here wondering where Chandra was right now."

"You're right. We should be grateful to this guy,"

Sebastian conceded with a nod. "I'm really glad you're okay, sis."

"Thank you, Sebastian." Chandra gave her wrist a reprieve from the ice.

"The fact that the guy is a tall, dark and handsome drink of water that sis is totally into…" Naya shrugged with a grin. "That's just a happy bonus."

His youngest daughter's comment drew various responses from her older brothers and a whispered "Snitch" from her sister. Ray chuckled. He missed having all of his children together like this. Even missed their petty bickering. Because they only did it because they loved each other.

Ray draped an arm around Chandra and lowered his voice. "So you really like this fella, hmm?"

"He was nice. Sweet even. And yes, he was handsome. So yeah, I guess I do like him a little in a passing fancy sort of way." Chandra shrugged.

"You do realize that no one says 'passing fancy' anymore, right?" Naya leaned over the seat, poking her head of pink hair between his and Chandra's, just like when she was a little girl and would eavesdrop on their conversations.

"And you do realize this was a private conversation?" Chandra shot back.

Naya shrugged, then sauntered off.

Ray shook his head and laughed.

"As I was saying, yeah, maybe I have a crush on the guy. But it's nothing serious. Besides, he lives here, and I don't." Chandra shrugged her shoulders. "End of story." She dropped the ice wrap on the table and stood. "I'm starving. I'm gonna grab something to eat." She indicated the platters of sandwich fixings her brothers were already attacking. Dejah had just set them on the sideboard. "Want anything?"

Ray waved a hand and sighed quietly. He topped off his drink and took a sip.

Maybe this town could deliver the two things he wanted most. To build a legacy of his own for his family and to see his children find the happily-ever-after that had always eluded him.

Six

Julian pulled the borrowed truck into the gravel driveway of his mother's house and turned off the engine. Her small red import was parked near the entrance to her prized garden beds. Gardening was the one thing that still seemed to bring his mother joy since his father's death twenty years ago.

He stepped out of the truck, not bothering to grab his luggage. He wouldn't be staying here. The deal to return home to Magnolia Lake as the local doctor included accommodations and the use of a vehicle.

Julian shielded his eyes from the glaring afternoon sun as he surveyed the unassuming little white cottage. The house and the white picket fence surrounding it had recently been painted.

Fall flowering bushes and late-blooming perennials added pops of color to the stark white structure and lent warmth and curb appeal to the one-hundred-year-old house. His father had purchased the dilapidated, abandoned structure before Julian was born and remodeled it bit by bit.

Julian sometimes wondered how his mother had managed to stay in the old house all these years. Every room, every surface echoed with memories of his father—a large, amiable man with dark gleaming eyes, a contagious smile and a deep, rumbling laugh.

"Plan on coming inside?"

Julian's gaze met the dark eyes that were a carbon copy of his own. His eyes and nose he'd gotten from Luetta Brandon. Yet in all the essential ways he'd been the spitting image of his dad.

It was undoubtedly why there was so much pain in his mother's eyes whenever she'd looked at him. It must've been like seeing the ghost of his dad plastered on the face of the person she blamed for his death.

"Hey, Ma." Julian crept forward. "The house looks great. When'd you have it painted?"

"Earlier this year. Also had the kitchen and bathrooms updated." His mother pulled off her gardening gloves and shoved them in the pocket of her apron.

They shared their obligatory hug. Only, this time his mother held on to him a little longer. It reminded him of the warm hugs she'd given him as a kid.

"You didn't mention that you were having work done. I could've painted the place for you." He'd done it twice before in the twelve years since he'd moved away.

"I know you would've. But you're a busy doctor now, Jules. You barely have time to spend with your mother as it is."

First shot fired.

But to be honest, he'd had it coming.

Julian communicated with his mother regularly but avoided coming home, convinced neither of them enjoyed suffering through awkward holiday weekends together. Had he simply been projecting his own feelings onto her so he'd feel less guilty about staying away?

"Sorry I haven't been home in a while, Ma. I guess I was trying to—"

"Get in all the adventures you could before you had to come back here?" She studied him. "Magnolia Lake isn't a prison."

"I know. But I'd be lying if I said I wasn't going to miss the conveniences of city life."

"Conveniences?" She tugged on his beard. "Like a good barber? Because we have those here, mountain man." She chuckled. "Almost didn't recognize who it was out here lurking in my yard. I was about five seconds away from loading my rifle."

Welcome to the "Julian Brandon can't do shit right" show.

"I've been here like five minutes, Ma. Can we save the discussion of my questionable life choices for the hour mark?" he suggested, only half teasing.

"Unfortunately, an hour is all I have." She glanced at her watch—a tenth anniversary gift from his father. She was hardly ever without it. "I volunteered to take the evening shift. Everyone else has children or grandchildren to see about."

She made the statement matter-of-factly. Still, guilt churned in his gut.

His mother was a nurse in the maternity ward of a

premier hospital in Gatlinburg. When he was a kid, she'd wanted him to grow up to be a doctor. At the time, his only interest was in being a superhero or a firefighter. But the day Joseph Abbott had asked him what he wanted to be when he grew up, his response had been immediate. He wanted to be a doctor.

It felt like his best shot at getting his mother to forgive him for destroying their lives.

Somewhere along the way, he'd come to enjoy being a doctor. He found recompense in being there for people on what was often the worst day of their lives.

"Sorry, I'd planned to get here earlier, but…" Chandra's lovely face flashed in his brain and his mouth curved in an involuntary smile. "I stumbled across an accident and stopped to help. Turned out it was the passenger I sat beside on the plane."

"It's the same thing your father would've done." There was a hint of pride in her dark eyes. "Probably didn't hurt that she was pretty either."

"How'd you know…?"

"I'm still your mother, Julian Aurelius Brandon," she reminded him. "The twinkle in your eyes and that sly little smile were a dead giveaway. She local?"

"No, she's in town because her father asked her and her siblings to meet him at the Richardson Winery. He was kind of mysterious about it, so she was worried."

"The Richardson Vineyards is now the Valentine Vineyards. The Richardsons sold the place a few weeks ago," his mother informed him. "The woman you helped… was she a Valentine?" Luetta Brandon propped a fist on her hip.

"Possibly." Julian shrugged.

"Well, ain't that something." She glanced at her watch again. "You hungry? Got leftover pot roast and mashed potatoes from last night, if you've got time for a late lunch."

"Yes, ma'am. Of course."

His mother heated up the leftovers while he took a quick tour of the renovation that had breathed new life into the place. Then they sat down and ate, catching each other up on the basics of their lives. The conversation was superficial—the kind of things one might share with a stranger.

"I realize fancy accommodations are part of the deal," his mother said. "But this is still your home and there's plenty of space for you here."

Was she offering because she felt she should or because she genuinely wanted him there?

"Thanks, but coming home is already a big adjustment for me. Thought it'd be best if we each had our own space," Julian said.

"You're probably right." Her tight smile was unconvincing. She collected their plates.

The sadness in her voice gnawed at his gut. Maybe the offer was an olive branch—her way of making amends for her resentment of him in the past. A few years ago, that might've been enough. But he'd gone from that brokenhearted little boy desperate for his mother's approval to a man harboring resentments of his own. He wouldn't let her off that easily.

Julian stood. "I'd better go. I have to meet Joe and Duke Abbott at my new office in about fifteen minutes. But I'll see you soon."

"In case that fancy new place of yours doesn't come

with groceries." His mother handed him a bento box filled with leftovers.

Julian thanked his mother, then headed out to the truck. He drove into town and met Joseph Abbott, founder of the world-famous King's Finest Distillery, and his son Duke, the company's current CEO. He hadn't expected the brand-new, state-of-the-art office building. The Abbott family's gift to the town of Magnolia Lake.

Julian's new office was located on the second floor of the Abbott Medical Center. The building would eventually house dental offices and a pharmacy. *Dr. J. Brandon* was printed on the board in the lobby and on the door of his practice.

He'd been dreading his return home, but seeing his name on that door felt gratifying. He'd accomplished his goal, and the Abbotts were welcoming him back with open arms. Which made the request he was about to make of Joseph that much more difficult.

After a quick tour, Duke took off, saying he was on grandpa duty. As soon as he'd left, Joseph looked at Julian warily. Father Time and the stroke the old man had suffered a few years ago had aged him considerably. Made him look almost frail.

Joseph narrowed his dark eyes, framed by wiry gray brows. "Something is obviously weighing on you, son. Let's hear it."

The old man is still as sharp as ever.

Julian cleared his throat and stood taller. "Mr. Abbott... I appreciate everything you've done for me. And I'm prepared to fulfill my part of our agreement."

"But?" Joseph sat in one of the office chairs, his arms folded over his chest.

Julian sat beside the older man. "You made a financial investment in me, sir. I'd like to repay that debt… with interest." Julian pulled a check from his wallet and handed it to him.

Joseph Abbott rubbed his chin as he studied the six-figure check. "You want to repay me in lieu of serving your four years as town doctor?"

"Yes, sir."

"No." The old man handed the check back to him. "I don't need the money, son. But this town does need you. And maybe you need it, too."

Julian had hoped that Abbott would be tempted by the offer. But knowing what he did about the old man, his answer didn't surprise him.

"Should I be worried about where you got that kind of money?" Joseph asked.

"No. I worked for every penny. Started off flipping properties with a few buddies. Then I got into real estate investment and stock market investment."

"You've been busy." Joseph sounded like a proud father. But then he grimaced. "Being able to buy your way out of this agreement must've been pretty damn important to you."

"Yes, sir. It was."

"Why, son?" Joseph asked.

"I've built a good life in Philly," Julian said.

"And what about Lue?" the old man asked.

Julian sighed heavily, the guilt over his relationship with his mother weighing on him. He ran a hand over his head. "I love my mother. But you know how things have been between us." He shrugged. "Me coming back here… It'll only churn up painful memories for both of us."

"Your mother loves you very much, and folks around here are awful glad you're back. As for those memories… I think you'll find that facing them head-on is far more effective than trying to outrun them."

The old man's words hit Julian squarely in the chest. Outrunning painful memories was exactly what he'd tried to do for years now. Yet they haunted him at every turn. So maybe Joseph was right.

"I've been a man of my word—now I expect you to be the same." Joe climbed to his feet. He pulled an envelope from his inside jacket pocket. "Inside you'll find the address to your cabin and three sets of keys. One to this office. One to the cabin. One for the vehicle parked in the drive. The cabin is fully stocked, and your staff is all set and eager to work with you. Need anything else? Don't hesitate to give me a call."

Julian accepted the envelope and nodded. "Thank you, Mr. Abbott. For everything."

The old man patted Julian's arm and smiled. Then he took off.

Julian surveyed his fancy new office, hoping the old man was right about his coming back home being a good move.

He locked up the office and headed for Old Man Simpson's farm to deliver the truck. But he couldn't help thinking about Chandra—the intriguing woman he'd met on the plane.

Julian hoped things had gone well in her meeting with her dad and siblings. But most of all, he hoped he'd get to see Chandra again before she left town with his favorite shirt.

If he was lucky, he'd get to see Chandra in that shirt again—and not much else.

Seven

It'd been two days since her father had stunned Chandra and her siblings with the news of his true paternity, the fact that they were cousins of the Abbotts—owners of the world-renowned King's Finest Distillery—and also apparently the owners of the run-down old Richardson Winery.

Chandra flexed her wrist, which was still sore and incapable of bearing weight. She figured it would be fine, but her dad insisted someone look at it. Then he'd tasked Dejah with making an appointment with the town doctor. Chandra glanced over at the younger woman who was transporting her into town for her appointment. They rode mostly in silence in the woman's beat-up old Jeep that was probably as old as she was.

Dejah Richardson—the youngest daughter of the vineyard's former owners—had agreed to stay on and work for Chandra's father. It explained Dejah's reserved demeanor. It couldn't have been easy watching someone else take over her family's business.

Chandra's father felt Dejah's help was invaluable, but she couldn't help being wary of Dejah's true motives for staying on at the vineyard.

"What made you decide to stay on at the winery when your family decided to sell?" Chandra asked.

Dejah's nostrils flared, her eyes not leaving the road. "I've been harvesting grapes and learning about winemaking since I was four. That winery has been my entire life." She shrugged. "Where else was I supposed to go?"

Anywhere.

Family businesses could be a blessing and a curse. Her father's situation was proof of that. Without the weight of family expectations, there were undoubtedly several options open to a smart, resourceful woman like Dejah. But she didn't know the woman or what she was looking for in life. Maybe there was something or someone keeping her in town.

Chandra wanted to ask, but the finality of the younger woman's answer made it clear she didn't want to discuss it further.

"Well, thank you for staying. My dad's heart is in the right place. I'm just not sure if he realizes exactly what he's gotten himself into." Chandra stared out the window as they passed over a river on a narrow one-car bridge. Then the colorful buildings of the quaint little town came into view.

"Here we are." Dejah parked in front of a building more modern than the quaint, colorful storefronts surrounding it. "The medical office is on the second floor. Doc Jules will get you all fixed up. I'll be back through here in about an hour and a half. I'll meet you at the Magnolia Lake Bakery across the street. If you get lost, call me."

Chandra thanked Dejah, then made her way to the second floor of the Abbott Medical Center and entered the offices of Dr. J. Brandon.

"Hello, I'm here to see Dr. Brandon about my wrist." Chandra held up her arm.

"The car accident." A pretty brunette woman shoved her fashionably colorful eyeglasses up her nose and nodded. "I'm glad that wrist is the only thing you hurt."

"Me, too." Chandra felt silly every time she had to recount running her rental into a ditch. She glanced around. Several pretty young women wielding some sort of basket or container occupied seats in the waiting room. "Is the doctor running behind schedule?"

"Not at all." The receptionist sounded offended. "Don't worry—Dr. Jules will get you all fixed up and out of here in no time." The woman handed Chandra a clipboard and pen. "*After* you finish your paperwork."

She accepted the clipboard, and once her paperwork was complete, a nurse called her name, right on time. After getting her vitals and following up on a few items, the older woman left her in the exam room to wait for Dr. Jules.

Chandra adjusted her position on the exam table, the paper crinkling in protest. Then she scanned her emails while she waited for the doctor.

A knock at the door startled Chandra.

"Come in," she said. But when she gazed up from

her phone, the face staring back at her didn't belong to the matronly physician she'd expected.

The baby-face doctor in a white coat with a stethoscope draped around his neck was incredibly handsome and surprisingly familiar. The sexy beard she'd admired on the plane was gone. But she'd recognize those dark eyes and devilish grin anywhere.

"Ms. Valentine. I see that wrist is still giving you trouble."

"JB?" She stared at him, blinking. "*You're* Dr. Jules?"

"Not the middle-aged white woman you were expecting, huh?" JB chuckled, his dark eyes twinkling. "Jules is a childhood nickname which has been unbelievably hard to shake. One of the hazards of returning to the little town you grew up in, I guess. I've been away for more than a decade, became a whole-ass doctor, and most of them still see me as Little Jules who got chased down Main Street by a baby goat."

Chandra's deep belly laugh alleviated the knot that had formed in her gut once she'd realized she'd been lusting over the town's child doctor. "You look...*different* without the beard."

"I know." JB rubbed his chin and sighed. "Did it as a favor to my mother. But I'm regretting that decision. The crotchety old mountain man look works for me, and it reminds folks around here that I'm not a mischievous kid anymore."

"No, of course not." She slipped her phone back into her purse and ran her fingers through her hair. "You're a mischievous adult now."

"Guilty." JB chuckled as he scrubbed his hands at the sink. The scent of the antiseptic soap filled the air.

Chandra couldn't help watching him. Even from behind, bent over a sink, this man was an absolute thing of beauty.

Her cheeks burned. For the past two days, she'd been daydreaming about her handsome, mysterious, bearded knight bending her over and taking her from behind. And now she just felt...*wrong*. And a little dirty. No, *a lot* dirty. Because he might technically be a grown-up and even a doctor. But he looked...*young*. Way too young for a woman who was nearly forty.

Thank God she hadn't taken him up on his offer to call her if she needed...*anything*. So maybe she'd had a few erotic thoughts about the handsome doctor. They hadn't actually done anything, so she had nothing to feel guilty about.

"All right, Ms. Valentine. Let's take a look at that wrist."

The rest of the appointment went as expected. He called her Ms. Valentine. She called him Dr. Brandon. Chandra tried to ignore the spread of warmth through her skin as he gently handled her wrist to examine it. She managed to restrain herself from sliding off the exam table and straddling his lap as he sat on the rolling leather stool.

After all, she wasn't some sex-starved vamp who was desperate for the man.

Okay, maybe she was sex starved...and kind of desperate for this man—but she was certainly not a vamp.

"Ms. Valentine?" JB looked slightly amused, and she had the feeling he'd had to call her name more than once.

Chandra's face heated. "Yes, Doctor?"

"I asked if your rental car has been replaced." He washed his hands again.

"There are several cars between my dad and siblings. So I don't really need one. Besides, with my wrist being sore, I'd rather not drive."

"How'd you get into town?"

"Dejah Richardson dropped me off on her way to get some supplies. She's meeting me at the café across the way in—" Chandra glanced down at her watch "—about an hour."

"Then you're in good hands. Say hello to Dejah for me." His eyes lingered on hers. Warmth spread through her skin. Her belly fluttered.

What was it about Dr. Julian Brandon that made her feel like a teenager with a crush?

"We'll do a quick X-ray, just to make sure none of the small bones in your wrist have been damaged." He folded his arms and leaned against the counter. "If this is a mild sprain, as I suspect, the ligaments in your wrist probably got stretched while you were gripping the wheel during your accident. We'll wrap your wrist and have you follow the RICE protocol—rest, ice, compression, elevation. A little ibuprofen, when needed. Follow those guidelines and you'll be good as new in no time."

"Thank you, Doctor," she called to his retreating back.

He gave her a brief nod and exited the room.

Chandra hadn't wanted JB to flirt with her now that she realized he was far too young for her. Still, she couldn't help feeling a little insulted. His all-business demeanor and sudden lack of interest likely had everything to do with him seeing her age on her chart.

After her X-rays, the doctor wrapped her wrist, said his goodbyes, and then his nurse went over the care protocol with Chandra before directing her back to the reception desk.

A pretty redhead approached the receptionist while Chandra was digging for her credit card.

"I've been sitting here *forever,*" the redhead complained, clutching her small wicker basket. "How is it that everyone else manages to get seen?" The woman cast an angry gaze at Chandra.

"Because they made appointments for actual medical issues. They didn't just pop in for an unscheduled social call with the doctor. And as I said, I can understand if you don't have time to wait until he's free. I'd be happy to deliver the—"

"No." The woman shifted the basket away from the receptionist's outstretched arms. "I'd like to deliver this to Jules myself, if you don't mind."

"Up to you." The receptionist—Lindee, according to her name tag—shrugged. "But you'll need to wait a bit longer while he sees actual patients. If you don't mind," Lindee said with a smirk.

The redhead huffed off, her heels clicking against the tile floor.

"Sorry about that." Lindee turned back to Chandra. "Dr. Jules has become Magnolia Lake's most eligible bachelor since his return." She indicated the women seated in the waiting room clutching various gifts.

"Who did he displace?" Chandra asked.

"The previous reigning champion, Cole Abbott, who surprised us all and got engaged a few months ago."

Of course.

Chandra glanced at the door that led to the doctor's office. So much for her fantasies about her knight in shining armor.

Julian slipped into his office to check his messages. He peered out the window as Chandra crossed the street. He'd wanted to greet her with a hug, as they had when they'd parted at the winery. But she was there to see him in his official capacity as the town's doctor, so it didn't feel appropriate.

He was startled by a gentle knock on his open door. Lindee—his receptionist and a childhood friend—stepped forward, a wide smile on her face. "Hey, Jules. We had two last-minute cancellations. Your next patient isn't until after lunch. Would you like to start seeing the ladies waiting for you in the lobby?"

No, he wouldn't. He'd much prefer to be sipping coffee with the intriguing Ms. Valentine.

He glanced out the window again. "Actually, I need to step out. I won't be more than an hour. Please offer again to accept the baskets on my behalf. If they'd prefer to wait, I'll see them when I get back."

"But I—"

"I'll bring back a box of those bear claws you like so much." Julian stripped off the white coat and hung it on the back of the door. Then he hurried out the back door, rather than going through the waiting room.

Julian jogged over to the Magnolia Lake Bakery. He paused for a moment to catch his breath, then approached the counter as Chandra placed her order.

Chandra was wearing a simple short flared black skirt, a white blouse and a gray wool coat. Her dark brown hair fell in soft curls over one shoulder. The smooth brown skin of her legs shimmered. And that subtle honeysuckle scent that had grabbed him the moment he'd sat beside her on the plane seemed to drift in the air, reminding him of playing in the backyard with his dad when he was a kid.

"You can add that to my order," Julian said, when Chandra reached inside her purse for her wallet.

The cashier looked to Chandra for confirmation. She gave the younger woman a reluctant nod, then turned to him, her arms folded.

"I feel like we need to start over again here," Julian said, taking in Chandra's cocked hip and skeptical expression. He extended a hand. "I'm Dr. Julian Brandon, hometown boy slash prodigal son. JB is what most people outside this town have called me since college."

"Chandra Valentine." She shook his offered hand, still regarding him suspiciously. "Tell me, do you treat all of your patients to lunch, Dr. Jules?"

Damn, he really wished she hadn't gotten wind of that nickname. He'd been trying to ditch it since he was ten. Slapping *Doctor* on the front of it didn't do much to make it better.

"Just the really beautiful ones who sustain wrist injuries while trying to avoid a bear."

And just like that, her determined frown turned into an adorable smirk.

He ordered a sandwich and coffee. When the cashier asked if it was for there or to go, Julian turned to Chandra.

"Here," Chandra said. Once they were seated in a

booth, she folded her hands on the table. "Thank you for lunch."

"Thank you for accepting my invitation."

"Is that what that was?" Her eyes flickered.

"Okay, it was an *implied* invitation." He leaned forward, his arms folded on the table as he drank her in.

Chandra was more gorgeous every time he saw her.

She dropped her gaze, as if embarrassed by his stare. "Isn't there some rule about doctors and their patients—"

"Having lunch?" Julian shrugged, barely able to hold back a grin. "None that I recall."

"You know what I mean, *Doogie Howser*." Chandra pointed a finger. "You must be all of…what? Twenty-five?"

"*Et tu*, Chandra?" He'd been in town a few days and had heard his fair share of references to the fictional child doctor. Otherwise, he wouldn't have known who Doogie Howser was. "I'm thirty. Thirty-one on my birthday in a few months."

"I'm nearly old enough to be your mother," she muttered.

Julian tried his best to hide his amusement.

"You're nowhere close to my mother's age. Besides, I've dated women older than you." He shrugged. "The age difference doesn't bother me. As for your question about the doctor-patient relationship… If we'd met in my exam room, I wouldn't be sitting here. But our relationship clearly predates any doctor-patient connection."

"I wasn't aware we had a *relationship*." Chandra leaned forward, her elbow on the table and her chin propped on the fist of her uninjured hand. Her rich brown eyes studied him.

"Well, you did hold my hand on the plane," he reminded her. "In some cultures, that's practically a marriage proposal."

"True. But neither of us is from such a culture." Her full lips curved in a reluctant smile.

Julian had the sudden urge to glide his fingers into the nape of Chandra's neck and tug her forward, so he could sample the berry-tinted gloss on her lips.

"Then there's that hug you gave me," he continued, ignoring her earlier objection.

"That was a show of gratitude. You saved my life."

Someone would've come along and extracted her from the vehicle, and she certainly wasn't in danger of death. But now, while he was trying to convince her to go out with him, probably wasn't the best time to bring that up.

"I'm just saying…after the thirty-second mark, I'm pretty sure the hug went from gratitude to something… *more*." Julian chuckled when she huffed indignantly. "What? Is it so terrible to admit you're attracted to me?"

"No. I mean…yes." Chandra looked adorably flustered. "Maybe I was attracted to you. But—"

"Great. Because the attraction is mutual." Julian leaned in slightly and lowered his voice. "The Universe keeps throwing us together, Chandra. Seems like a glaring sign it's best not to ignore."

"So now our meeting was destiny or something?" Chandra furrowed her brows.

"Or something." He grinned.

The server brought a chicken club for her and hot pastrami for him.

"This sandwich is delicious," Chandra declared after a few minutes of eating in awkward silence.

"The food here is always amazing."

"What about at the King's Finest Family Restaurant?" Chandra asked.

"The place just opened a few weeks ago. I ate there for the first time last night. The Blake's Steak was phenomenal. Not surprising though." He shrugged. "The Abbotts don't do anything half-assed."

"You know them?" Something shifted in her demeanor at the mention of Magnolia Lake's first family.

"Around here, they're practically royalty." Julian chuckled.

"But what you said speaks to a closer relationship with the family. You don't just know them by reputation," Chandra noted.

"You could say that." He set down the remainder of his sandwich and wiped his hands. "Joseph Abbott paid for my education."

"That was generous." Chandra took another bite of her sandwich. "Was it a town scholarship?"

"It was sort of my personal deal with the Devil." Julian laughed when Chandra's eyes went wide. "Don't get me wrong—Joseph Abbott is a great guy. But he's used to getting his way. He didn't get where he is in life without knowing how to turn a few screws to get people to do exactly what he wants."

"And what did he want from you?" Chandra asked.

He studied her brown eyes, brimming with curiosity. He was glad she was interested but couldn't help wondering why.

"He wanted me to come back here and become the town's doctor once Doc Johnson was ready to retire."

"For the rest of your life?"

"He's not *that* persuasive," Julian said. "He asked for an eight-year commitment. We settled on four."

"You proposed the deal?"

"No." Julian rubbed his neck. "Let's just say he made me an offer I couldn't refuse, so I made the most of it."

Chandra leaned in closer. "Did they threaten you?"

"Yes. Joe Abbott threatened my bad ass with jail for stealing his Mercedes and taking it for a joyride."

"You *stole* his car?" She whispered the offending word. "How old were you?"

Julian sighed, abandoning his sandwich again. He licked honey Dijon mustard from his thumb and Chandra's eyes darkened. His body responded and he was more than a little glad they were seated at a table.

"I was fourteen and not at the best place in my life." He frowned, thinking about his life then.

"Why?" Chandra's warm hand covered his.

"Why did I steal his car or why was I at a bad place in my life?"

"Both," she said, without hesitation.

He'd already divulged more of his personal history to Chandra than he had with any woman he'd been interested in. Normally, he pulled away or simply changed the subject when a topic came up he didn't want to discuss. A few relationships had ended because he hadn't been willing to open up about his past.

So why was he telling Chandra Valentine, whom he barely knew, his pitiful life story?

Maybe because he was back in Magnolia Lake, where

his story was common knowledge. Chandra was bound to find out if she asked the right person, and he'd rather she hear it from him. Or maybe it was because he'd do just about anything to keep her there with him, her warm skin covering his.

"I told you my dad died in a car crash when I was a kid." His mouth suddenly felt dry. The words just wouldn't seem to come. This was something he hadn't talked about in ages. Since he stopped going to therapy years ago.

His hands involuntarily tensed. But rather than withdrawing her hand from his, Chandra slid her fingers into his palm, comforting him the way he'd comforted her on the plane.

It was always embarrassing to tell this story. But there was something about Chandra that put him at ease. Like he could trust her with his truth—no matter how ugly it was.

"My mom and I…neither of us handled my dad's death well. She kind of checked out, and my bright idea to get her attention was to act out. I did an escalating variety of stupid things to get into trouble, hoping she'd snap out of it."

Chandra stroked the back of his closed fist with her thumb. His grip loosened and his shoulders relaxed.

"That must've been really tough for both of you." Her gaze lowered to their connected hands. "My mother walked away when I was eight. My stepmother ditched us when I was fourteen. Both times, I spiraled into this dark place, believing there must be something wrong with me because neither of them stuck around. I felt lost and didn't always make the best decisions. It didn't mean I was a bad person." She met his gaze and smiled softly. "And Joseph Abbott evidently saw the good in you."

"I guess he did." Julian sighed. "He gave me a choice. If I planned to continue on the 'road to ruin,' he'd save me some time and make sure my ass ended up in juvie. Option two—if I was willing to work hard for it, he'd help me become anything I wanted to be. I told him fine, I wanted to be a doctor."

Julian chuckled recalling the old man's expression. *You sure do swing for the fences, don't you, son?*

"That was quite a commitment." Chandra released his hand and picked up her sandwich. A soft smile lit her eyes. "Bet he wasn't expecting that."

"He definitely wasn't. But he kept his word. Gave me a free ride to college and then medical school. In return, I agreed to serve as the town's doctor for at least four years once old Doc Johnson retired. A week ago, he finally did. That's why I'm here."

"So then you'd consider Joe Abbott a pretty trustworthy guy, then?" Chandra asked.

"I would." Julian folded his hands on the table. "Now I have a question. Why are you so interested in the Abbotts?"

Chandra set down her sandwich and folded her hands, too. "I found out what's going on with my dad. He's been going through sort of an identity crisis. After his mother's death a few years ago, he learned that he was adopted. He hadn't told any of us, but he joined one of those DNA ancestry registries, hoping to find his real family."

"Your father is related to Joe Abbott?" Julian asked.

"He's my dad's half brother. King Abbott was both their fathers, but they had different mothers. Joseph didn't know about my dad until recently. And my biological grandmother died a couple months after giving birth to my father. She knew she was going to die and asked that the family who adopted him keep his given name…Abbott."

"Which took on a hell of a lot more meaning once he discovered who he was related to." Julian whistled. "That must have come as quite a shock to all of you."

"It did. But the bigger shock was that he's selling the family textile business and has purchased the Richardson Vineyards. He has aspirations of building a wine empire that will rival his brother's bourbon empire."

"That's a tall order. Joe's been at this half a century," Julian said as diplomatically as he could.

"My dad swears it isn't a competition. But he discovered that King Abbott had hoped to branch out into wine-making. My dad and my brother Nolan have been amateur winemakers for years. The rest of us consume our fair share of it." She laughed nervously. "Guess Dad considers that enough of a reason to start a family-owned winery."

"None of you had any idea your dad had bought the winery?"

"Just my brother Nolan. And now Dad is asking us to drop our entire lives and move here to Green Acres… No offense," she added quickly.

"None taken. But for the record, the sitcom was called *Green Acres*. The town was Hooterville."

"How on earth would you know that?" She seemed

impressed. "That show was way before my time. It was definitely before yours."

"Syndication. Same as you." He grinned. "My mom always said I was an old soul."

"Which explains why you're asking me out when half a dozen beautiful women your age are probably still sitting in your waiting room bearing gifts."

"I'm not interested in any of them. I am *completely* taken with you. I have been since you nodded hello in that airport."

Why was there a weird fluttery feeling in his chest whenever he thought of that moment?

Her expression softened. She set down her sandwich. But before she could respond, her phone rang. "I'd better take this. It's Dejah."

He ate his sandwich while Chandra quickly chatted with Dejah Richardson.

"Dejah completed her errands quicker than expected. She's five minutes away. I have to go." Chandra stood.

Julian stood, too. "I know you won't be in town long, Chandra. But I'd love to see you again."

"Why?" She adjusted her purse strap on her shoulder. "Like you said, I won't be here long."

"I don't know." Maybe he was being too honest. It wasn't the most romantic appeal. "But I can't let go of the sense that you and I were meant to meet. I know that sounds—"

"Corny with a side of flower child?" She laughed.

"Something like that." Julian rubbed his chin.

"True. But it's also really sweet. It helps, of course, that you're cute, especially when you turn up the charm."

Julian grinned. "Is it working?"

"It would be," she said. "But my hands are pretty full right now. My dad is going through an identity crisis. It feels like each of my siblings is on the edge of some sort of personal crisis, too. And I'm this close to finally getting that corner office and the title and salary that go with it back in San Diego." She worried her lower lip with her teeth and frowned. "I can't afford any distractions right now, Julian. Not even one as handsome and charming as you."

He was interested. She wasn't. C'est la vie. He'd never be that asshole guy who wouldn't take no for an answer.

"Well, take care of that wrist, Ms. Valentine. And call me if you need…well…*anything*."

"Thank you, Dr. Brandon. And thank you for lunch. It was lovely getting to know you."

"You, too."

Julian groaned quietly as she turned and walked away.

He slipped back into the booth to finish his lunch, but he'd lost his appetite.

Maybe he should be more like Chandra and remain focused on his goal.

He'd committed to staying in Magnolia Lake for four years, and he'd do exactly that. Then his life would be his own, his obligation to the Abbotts and the town repaid.

Still, it was a shame she wouldn't be sticking around. Chandra Valentine was just the type of distraction that would make his time in Magnolia Lake go by more quickly.

Eight

Chandra stood in the middle of the barn where the Abbott family would be hosting a party for a couple hundred Magnolia Lake locals. The previous night, she and her siblings had met their father's half brother Joseph Abbott; his son and daughter-in-law, Duke and Iris Abbott; and all five of his grandchildren—Blake, Parker, Max, Cole and Zora, as well as their significant others, children and various in-laws, during a meal Iris hosted there.

Chandra and her brothers had been tense and unsure of what to expect. But Naya had walked in and hugged each of the Abbotts, as if she'd known them her entire life. Naya's relaxed attitude coupled with Zora's and Iris's warm and welcoming demeanor had eased any tensions between the two families.

The food—catered by the King's Finest Family

Restaurant—had been as amazing as Julian had said. They'd bonded over delicious food and classic soul: Marvin Gaye; Otis Redding; Aretha Franklin; Earth, Wind & Fire; Gladys Knight; and The Isley Brothers. By the end of the evening, the Abbotts felt like old friends—if not quite yet family. Even Sebastian's ever-present frown had eased a bit. Chandra wasn't sure if it was because Bas was actually having a good time or because he seemed taken with Parker's sister-in-law: his wife Kayleigh's older sister Evelisse.

Either way, it was nice to see her father happy, smiling and more at peace than she'd seen him in years. Nolan and Sebastian had actually let their guard down and enjoyed themselves. And she couldn't remember the last time she'd heard Alonzo, Nyles and Naya laugh so much. Seeing her family together and happy—something they hadn't been in so long—made her heart swell.

"So what do you think?" Blake's wife, Savannah, stood beside Chandra. Her adorable one-year-old daughter, Remi, whose hazel eyes were carbon copies of her mother's, was perched on Savannah's hip. "We went a little overboard, I know."

"No, not at all." Chandra tweaked the little girl's nose, and Remi giggled. The sound was pure joy, and it made Chandra smile. "The barn is stunning. Elegant and ethereal. It's like a winter wonderland."

"I know mid-October is way too early for Christmas decorations," Savannah said. "But country music star Dade Willis filmed his upcoming holiday special here. His team let us have the decorations, so we decided to keep them up and just roll with it."

"Everyone is going to love it, the kids especially," Chandra assured Savannah.

"Thanks, Chandra. We're thrilled you all are here. It's great seeing Grandpa Joe so happy." Savannah nodded toward the two newly minted half brothers. They were deep in animated conversation and clearly enjoying each other's company.

"My dad hasn't been this happy in a while," Chandra admitted. "Maybe never."

Savannah's gaze followed Chandra's as the barn door opened and a handful of guests filtered in. "Nervous about meeting the entire town?"

"A little." Chandra's shoulders tensed. "Not really looking forward to becoming the town curiosity."

"Folks can be a bit…*inquisitive*," Savannah conceded. They both laughed at her diplomatic way of saying *nosy*. "But they're good people. Warm and open. I'm originally from a little town in West Virginia, and I've only been here about five years. But Magnolia Lake feels like home now. It's a great place to live and raise a family." Savannah kissed her daughter's forehead.

For the briefest moment, Chandra thought about the wedding and family that didn't materialize for her five years ago. Edward, her ex, she didn't miss. But in fleeting moments, like this, she missed the *ideals* of marriage and motherhood. The realities of a husband and children…maybe not.

"I'm afraid my siblings and I are more inclined toward living in the city," Chandra said. "But Magnolia Lake is a lovely place to visit. I haven't been this relaxed in ages."

"I didn't move here with the intention of staying either. But then, I never planned on falling for this incredible guy." Savannah flashed a flirty smile at her husband, Blake, who was approaching.

There was so much love in both of their expressions. It almost felt as if Chandra was intruding on a private moment.

Blake leaned down and kissed his wife. He took their daughter, whose arms were outstretched to her father. Then he slipped an arm around Savannah's waist. "You coming here changed my life and started a chain reaction that changed our family and the company for the better."

Iris had told the story of how after Blake and Savannah had gotten married, it had seemingly created a domino effect, with each of her children finding their perfect mate, one by one. Chandra's father had quipped that his children seemed *determined* not to produce any grandchildren for him to spoil. And while he'd been teasing them, they all knew her dad was only half joking. He'd hoped that one of them would've given him a grandchild by now.

Blake grinned. "Four weddings down, one to go." He nodded toward where Cole and his fiancée, Renee, stood with her young son, Mercer.

Chandra had been struck by just how much Cole and Mercer seemed to adore each other. The sweet little boy was autistic and nonverbal, but it was clear just how much he loved Cole.

"Please, don't give my dad any ideas." Chandra laughed. She turned toward a familiar voice.

Dr. Julian Brandon.

She'd seen him in casual attire on the plane, titillating

gray sweats—the memory of which still made her body tingle—and his crisp white doctor's coat. But tonight's look was her favorite thus far.

Julian wore a handsome suit fitted perfectly to his athletic form. The suit, in an unexpected deep plum shade, looked good with the navy shirt he wore. The color of the suit was festive but not garish and popped nicely against his deep brown skin.

Chandra forced her attention back to Blake and Savannah, who both seemed to share a knowing smile.

"Anything I can do to help?" Chandra asked.

"Mingle and enjoy yourself." Savannah nodded in Julian's direction. "Your audience awaits."

Before she could think of a reply, Savannah and Blake were gone, leaving her there staring across the room at Julian. When their eyes met, his mouth curved in a lopsided smile, and he shoved one hand in his pocket, his gaze sliding down her body.

Chandra's face heated. She'd hoped that knowing Dr. Julian Brandon was too young for her would abate the deep attraction she felt for him. It hadn't. Now he wasn't just kind and devastatingly handsome. He was a tempting, forbidden morsel she couldn't stop thinking about.

As Julian moved in her direction, he was quickly cut off by three young women, one of whom was the redhead from his office the other day.

Chandra heaved a quiet sigh.

"Looks like your friend is the biggest thing to happen around these parts in a while." Naya approached her with a clear mug filled with what looked like hot apple cider. Her sister was wearing an adorable chinlength bob in a deep flame red. Her makeup—dramatic, yet tasteful—was festive and complemented her hair color nicely.

"It seems so." Chandra stared wistfully in Julian's direction, then indicated Naya's mug. "That smells good."

"It is." Naya handed her the mug.

Chandra sipped the heated beverage. The warmth and spicy sweetness washed over her tongue. The crisp taste of fall apples was followed by heat slowly building in her belly. She coughed a little. "There's liquor in this." She handed back the mug.

Naya laughed. "Lots of it. Cousin Zora was a little heavy-handed when she spiked the apple cider. But you won't hear me complaining about it."

"Duly warned." Chandra fanned her face.

Was the warmth surging through her from the unexpected shot of bourbon or seeing Julian in that suit that hugged his muscular body like a glove?

"Now, about your friend…" Naya gestured in his direction.

The crowd around him had gotten larger. Now there was an older woman standing with a younger woman who looked like her daughter. Even from this distance, it was obvious the woman was angling for a son-in-law.

"I feel sorry for Julian," Chandra said. "An entire night of fending off husband-hunters can't be much fun."

"Then what do you plan to do about it?" Naya asked.

"Me? Why do I need to do anything about it? It's not like we're involved."

"They don't know that," Naya noted. "The dude came to your aid *twice*." Naya held up two fingers. "Here's your chance to return the favor."

"And what exactly do you expect me to do?" Chandra turned toward her sister.

"Strut your fine ass over there and stake a claim on your man. Or, you know…your *pretend* man." She sipped her cider.

How many of those spiked apple ciders had her sister had? "You're suggesting that I pretend to be his girlfriend, *unsolicited*? I don't know, Nay. I'd love to help Julian out, but it isn't like he asked me to run interference."

"Look at the poor man. His eyes are *pleading* for help." Naya gestured toward him. "He rescued you from a bear-induced car accident. We cannot let him spend the evening miserable."

When Chandra didn't respond, Naya handed Chandra her mug and stood taller. She propped up her already perky breasts, then fluffed her wig.

"Fine. If you won't do it, I guess I'll have to. I'm going to walk right up to the baby doc and stick my tongue down his throat. That should send a pretty clear message."

"No!" Chandra's objection came out louder than she'd intended. She handed the mug back to Naya. "I'm the one indebted to him. I'll do it." She raked her fingers through her hair and straightened her shoulders.

Naya sipped her drink and grinned maniacally.

Manipulative little brat.

Chandra cut her eyes at Naya. "I hate you sometimes, you know that?"

"Love you, too, sis." Naya giggled. "Now let's see you work it. Show those little girls what's up." Naya slapped Chandra on the bottom and she jumped.

If this thing went sideways, Chandra was going to strangle her sister.

Chandra sucked in a deep breath, then walked to the other side of the room. She made her way through the crowd of women and touched Julian's arm.

"There you are, babe. I didn't realize you'd arrived." Chandra smiled sweetly, hoping he wasn't about to out her as a lunatic feigning a relationship.

Surprise flashed in his dark eyes, followed by an appreciative smile. He slipped a strong arm around her waist. She was reminded of when he'd lifted her from her car. Julian kissed her cheek and whispered, "Thanks, I owe you one."

"I just arrived," he said for the benefit of the women around him whose faces displayed varying degrees of disappointment. The redhead looked completely undone. "I was catching up with a few old friends."

"You two are dating?" The older woman who was standing with her daughter gestured between them. "That's news."

"I certainly haven't heard anything about you having a girlfriend." The redhead's tone was accusatory, as if there was some official town registry for dating couples.

"We met recently." Julian pulled her closer, not acknowledging either of them directly. "But the moment I laid eyes on Chandra—" a warm smile lit up his handsome face "—I knew she was the woman for me. Made it my mission to make her mine." He kissed her temple.

Chandra's skin tingled where Julian's body pressed to hers.

"I'm always nervous on those small regional planes. When we hit severe turbulence, I was scared out of my mind. Julian was so sweet and such a gentleman. I don't know how I would've made it through that flight without him." Their eyes locked and Chandra's stomach fluttered. "Julian took such good care of me. He held my hand through the worst of it."

"I'll bet he did," the redhead muttered.

The redhead's friend elbowed her, then extended a hand. "I'm Olivia Henderson. Folks call me Livvy. My aunt and uncle run the general store. I'm Benji and Sloane Bennett's nanny. Welcome to town…"

"Chandra. Chandra Valentine." She shook the woman's hand. "Nice to meet you, Livvy."

The rest of the women in the group introduced themselves, one by one, including the reluctant redhead, Deanna Jasper.

Finally, the crowd dissipated.

"I can't thank you enough." Julian uttered the words through clenched teeth and a smile, so only she could hear them. "You saved my ass."

"Thank my sister." She indicated Naya, who held up what Chandra was pretty sure was a fresh mug of spiked apple cider. "She suggested that rescuing you from the circling piranhas was the least I could do after all you've done for me. Besides, if I didn't, she threatened to prance over here and introduce her tongue to your tonsils. I figured I'd save us both the embarrassment."

Julian's deep chuckle rumbled through his chest. He lowered his voice. "Remind me to thank little sis."

A shiver ran down her spine. The space between her thighs pulsed and ached. She needed to get it together.

"Like I said, I owed you. Hopefully that sent the

message, and you won't be harassed the rest of the evening," Chandra said. "If there's someone here you are interested in, just tell them we broke up."

Julian rubbed the five-o'clock shadow on his strong jaw and smirked. "Sweetheart, you have no idea what you've just done, do you?"

"What do you mean?" Chandra glanced up at him.

"Ms. Adelaide—the older woman who was trying to marry off her daughter—is Magnolia Lake's walking, talking news bulletin."

"You mean the town gossip?" Chandra was beginning to feel like she was in Hooterville or perhaps Mayberry.

"Your words, not mine." Julian chuckled. "Ms. Adelaide will definitely spread the word about us. But if you think that little act alone will convince this crowd I'm off the market, you're mistaken." Julian's warm breath ghosted over her skin as he whispered in her ear. "Everyone here will be watching us all night."

Chandra glanced around the room. Several people were staring and whispering.

Why in the hell did she let Naya get her into these things?

No good deed goes unpunished.

It'd been a favorite phrase of her late grandmother's.

Chandra huffed. "My college drama teacher always said, 'Commit to the role.' I started this, so I'm in. I'll only be here another week and a half. Then you can say we're in a long-distance relationship for as long as you need to."

"Thanks, babe." Julian's eyes twinkled with amusement. He extended his large hand and she slid hers into it. "Heads up…the pissed-off woman marching in our direction is my mother."

What on earth have I gotten myself into?

Nine

Julian intertwined their fingers and glided his thumb over the back of Chandra's hand, hoping to ease the sudden tension rolling off her shoulders. "Just breathe."

Chandra sucked in a deep breath, her hand trembling. She pressed her lips—painted a deep, enticing shade of wine—into a tentative smile. "Commit to the role," she muttered quietly.

"Hey, Ma. Didn't realize you'd arrived." Julian kissed his mother's cheek but didn't release Chandra's hand. "There's someone I really want you to meet. This is—"

"You must be Chandra Valentine." His mother ignored him. She extended a hand to Chandra and offered a stiff smile. "I've heard so much about you...*in the last five minutes.*"

"It's a pleasure to meet you, Mrs. Brandon," Chandra said. "Julian has told me so much about you."

His mother's expression softened. She seemed to appreciate that Chandra had called her *Mrs.* Brandon. "Some of it good, I hope." His mother finally spared him a glance.

"All of it good," Chandra lied, which he appreciated. "He tells me you're a nurse in the maternity ward at a hospital in Gatlinburg."

"Yes, I am." His mother seemed puzzled as she glanced between them.

"He admires the work you've done. Even more so as a single mother. I was so moved to learn that your work as a nurse is what prompted Julian to become a doctor. You must be really proud of him and thrilled he's finally back home."

His mother blinked, seemingly stunned.

Chandra had defused the fire in Luetta Brandon's eyes and turned the woman into a puddle of goo. She'd have to teach him that trick.

"You never told me that me being a nurse is the reason you became a doctor," his mother said.

"I just assumed you knew."

Julian was glad his mother wasn't lighting into him—especially since he had it coming. She couldn't have been happy about Ms. Adelaide making her feel like she was the very last to know about his "relationship" with Chandra. But having this conversation about why he became a doctor was uncomfortable. As were the raw feelings and bitter memories the revelation invoked. Especially here in front of his fake girlfriend in whom he was *seriously* interested.

"I didn't." There was a hint of sadness in her voice. "I guess that's one more thing we need to talk about."

His mother cleared her throat and returned her attention to the woman clutching his hand. "Well, it's nice to finally meet you, Chandra."

"And it was a pleasure to meet you, Mrs. Brandon." Chandra sounded more confident. "I'm sorry we didn't get a chance to meet before now, but the past few days have been a whirlwind, meeting my new cousins and learning about the winery."

"I can imagine." His mother pulled her black sequined cardigan tight around her shoulders. "And please, friends call me Lue." She turned to Julian. "I realize you're both busy, but I hope my son finds time to bring you by the house for lunch. How long are you staying in town?"

"A week and a half. Then I have to get back to San Diego."

"That's a shame." His mother frowned. "Folks around here are hoping that you'll all put down roots and become part of the community, like the Richardsons were."

"Magnolia Lake is a charming town, and everyone I've met has been really lovely. Now that my dad is moving here, you won't be able to keep us away," Chandra assured her.

"Good," his mother said. "Now, I should make the rounds. I'll see you two later."

"Of course," Julian said.

"Looking forward to it." Chandra smiled sweetly.

"You realize you defused a live bomb just now, right?" Julian slid his arm around Chandra's waist. "What is it you do for a living again? Because if what you just did isn't part of it, your gift is being wasted."

Chandra laughed, leaning into him. "Essentially? I babysit grown-ass folks who behave like toddlers and do whatever it takes to get them to either actually do their jobs or find somewhere that might be more suitable for them. Even if that's the couch in front of their TV at home."

"You're a hatchet woman. No wonder your job has you so tense." He turned her around and placed his hands on her tight shoulders, gently kneading the corded muscles there.

Chandra purred and the sound went directly below his belt. He couldn't stop imagining having this stunningly beautiful woman beneath him as she made the same sound, their fingers threaded above her head.

"Get a room, you two." Chandra's younger sister—*Maya? Or maybe Naya?*—grinned.

"*You're* the one who got us into this." Chandra pointed an accusatory finger.

Julian mouthed the words *thank you* and winked.

Chandra's sister laughed again. "Anyway, Savannah sent me over here to tell you she made room at our table for your new beau here and his mom."

Chandra sighed. "This just keeps getting better."

"Agreed," Julian said. Though he meant it literally, while she was clearly being sarcastic. "I'll let my mother know."

"You realize what this means?" Chandra turned to him after her sister walked away. "We're going to have to sit through a bunch of awkward questions about our relationship, which isn't a relationship, while…while…"

"Holding hands, cuddling and showing borderline

inappropriate amounts of PDA?" Julian chuckled. "I'm *totally* down with that."

Chandra huffed, though there was a hint of amusement in her eyes. "You're getting a kick out of this, aren't you?"

"I am." Julian stepped closer and looped his arms around her waist as he gazed down into those dark brown eyes that had captured him the moment they'd locked on to his. "Aren't you?"

"You're beneath the mistletoe." Nannette Henderson, owner of the general store in town, pointed above their heads.

"So we are." Julian smiled at Chandra.

"But it's nowhere close to being Christmas," Chandra objected.

"I don't make the rules, sweetie." Mrs. H shrugged. "Didn't hang the mistletoe in the middle of October either."

Julian smiled at Chandra. He leaned down slowly, providing ample opportunity for her to object if she didn't want to be kissed. She erased the remaining space between them and pressed her mouth to his.

Chandra's lips were soft and supple. Her mouth tasted like apples and bourbon. And her warm curves molded to his body.

Julian forced himself to pull back, wishing they were somewhere more private.

"Well." Mrs. H fanned herself. "That was *some* kiss. Seems you two are the real deal...not that I ever doubted it," she added quickly. Mrs. H hurried over to Ms. Adelaide— who'd undoubtedly put her up to the stunt.

"You think that'll keep them at bay?" Chandra flashed Ms. Adelaide a cheeky smile.

"Maybe for about an hour." Julian chuckled, taking her hand again. "C'mon. There's a town full of people eager to meet you."

Julian leaned against one of the posts, a glass of mulled cider in his hand. He tried not to stare at Chandra, but whenever she wasn't by his side, her hand tucked in his, he found himself searching the room for her. He studied every delicious curve on her tantalizing frame.

Who knew a sweaterdress could be so damn sexy? The deep V-neck of the belted red dress offered a hint of cleavage. The hem fell an inch or two above her knees, and a side split exposed the smooth, deep brown skin of one mouthwatering thigh. Her dangling silver earrings matched her belt and the glittering silver stiletto heels made her legs look a mile long. He had an unhealthy obsession with the idea of those shoes dangling over his shoulders as he kissed his way up her inner thigh.

Down, boy. Down.

Chandra might've been amenable to a kiss for the sake of warding off the group of women who seemed fascinated with him since his return. But since she'd turned down his request for a date, taking her to bed probably wasn't in the cards for them.

Still, he was enjoying their little charade more than he should. Every touch of her hand. The warmth of her skin as they stood together with his arm around her waist. The taste of her soft, sweet lips when he'd kissed her beneath the mistletoe. Chandra Valentine had a gift for driving him wild.

Even as they sat beside each other at the table, their parents grilling them, he enjoyed being with Chandra and getting to know her and her family.

The twins—Naya and Nyles—were a hot mess but entertaining. Nolan was fairly quiet but seemed to be constantly observing everyone and everything. Sebastian had spent most of the night frowning at him, and Alonzo was definitely a ladies' man. Her father, Abbott—who went by his middle name, Ray—was warm and friendly, but clearly assessing him. Deciding whether he measured up to his daughter.

Still, he was enjoying every single moment with her.

"You're *really* into my cousin, aren't you?" Cole stood beside him, a beer bottle in his hand. "Don't even try to deny it." Cole chuckled before Julian could open his mouth to object. "Got that damn goofy grin on your face. You're in heaven."

"So, apparently, are you." Julian nodded toward Cole's fiancée, Renee, who was twirling her son on the dance floor, to the boy's delight.

"Yeah." Cole's eyes lit up. "I am."

"I'm surprised Milo Lockwood didn't object to Magnolia Lake's notorious bad boy dating his granddaughter." Julian nodded toward the older man who was dancing with his wife to "For the Love of You" by The Isley Brothers.

"Object? I'm pretty sure the old goat tricked us into it." Cole chuckled. "And I could kiss the old bastard for it."

Cole Abbott was a few years older than Julian. But he was the Abbott sibling Julian was most familiar with.

He'd gotten to know Cole while working as a laborer for Milo's construction company one summer. Who knew Cole would go on to start his own real estate development company and achieve all he had? He usually grabbed a beer with Cole whenever he returned to town and they'd met up a couple of times when Cole had come to Philly.

Julian had been stunned to learn his friend had settled down and was about to become a stepfather.

"Legendary badass Cole Abbott is putting down roots. Wow, I feel like I'm in the *Twilight Zone* right now. You'd tell me if we were in a parallel universe, right?"

"Shut up, *Jules*." Cole nudged Julian with his elbow but laughed. "Times change and people mature." He shrugged. "Ren and I found each other again at the right time. And I honestly couldn't be happier."

"I'm happy for you, man. Seriously. Congrats." Julian held up his mug of mulled cider and Cole tapped it with his half-finished bottle of beer. "When's the big day?"

"Next summer," Cole said, with a goofy grin of his own. He turned to him. "But enough about me. What's up with you and my cousin? I'm not gonna have to kick your ass, am I?"

"You two have been related for like five minutes," Julian noted. "We've been boys for over a decade, and it's like that?"

"Family is family. So don't do anything stupid," Cole warned.

Like pretend dating?

"I really like Chandra." Julian glanced at her wistfully. "So don't worry. I'm pretty sure I'm the one who'll end up with a broken heart."

"Then here's hoping it works out for both of you." Cole held up his fist and Julian bumped it with his own.

Cole joined his fiancée and her son on the dance floor. Mercer could barely contain his excitement as Cole approached, and Julian couldn't help feeling the tiniest bit of envy.

Suddenly, the opening strains of McFadden & Whitehead's "Ain't No Stopping Us Now" began to play. The DJ encouraged everyone to form a Soul Train Line.

Julian went over to Chandra, who was chatting with Max Abbott and his wife, Quinn. After apologizing for the interruption, he slipped an arm around her waist and asked her to join him on the dance floor.

"I haven't done a Soul Train Line in years." Chandra gazed at the dance floor longingly.

It wasn't a no. She just needed some encouragement.

"Great idea," Quinn said. "C'mon, Max. Let's join them."

They went through the Soul Train Line twice. There was something about Chandra's genuine joy and laughter that made his chest swell. The sway of her generous hips in that sweaterdress made other parts of his anatomy swell, too.

When "Be Ever Wonderful" by Earth, Wind & Fire came on, he clutched her hand. "Dance with me?"

Chandra's eyes glittered beneath the twinkling lights strung along the overhead beams. She stepped into his arms as they swayed together.

"Have I told you how incredible you look?" Julian asked.

"A time or two. Not that I mind hearing it again."

Chandra's bashful grin made his pulse race. "So thank you."

"Thank you for stepping in to save me earlier. It was an extremely pleasant surprise."

"It was the least I could do. Besides, there are worse things than spending the next seven days on the arm of a handsome doctor who rescues nervous flyers and accident victims." Her sweet smile lit up the entire room.

Why did his heart swell and his pulse race every time she looked at him like that?

"The night sky here is so gorgeous." Chandra nodded toward the barn door, which opened when someone stepped outside. "I miss how bright the stars appeared in the night sky when I was a kid. The city lights dim the brilliance of the stars."

"Light pollution." Julian nodded. "I love city life, but I did miss seeing the stars. When I was a kid, my dad bought me a telescope and he'd point out the constellations. It was our thing." Julian hadn't thought of those nights under the stars with his dad in so long.

When the song ended, he didn't release Chandra and she didn't pull away. He stared at her a moment.

"There's something you should see. Wanna get out of here?"

Chandra studied him a moment, then slid her hand in his.

Ten

"This is quite an upgrade," Chandra noted, surveying the brilliant blue Audi e-tron Premium Plus quattro SUV the valet pulled up in. It was one of the models she'd considered before she'd purchased her black BMW X3.

"Part of the package." Julian helped her inside, then tipped the valet.

"What is it that you want to show me?" Chandra asked after they'd pulled onto the road.

"It's a surprise. But you'll like it. Promise."

Chandra had spent the evening dancing with Julian, holding his hand, even kissing him. She'd reminded herself time and again it was just an act and that he was too young for her. But that hadn't stopped her belly from fluttering or the sparks of electricity from dancing along her skin.

"How are you adjusting to meeting your new family and discovering that you're now part owner of a winery?" Julian's eyes didn't leave the road. "It's a lot to take in."

The concern in his voice reminded Chandra of why she'd been so drawn to him when he'd comforted her on the plane.

"It's been a roller coaster of emotions. I'm still worried my dad made a rash, impulsive decision in buying the place. But I can't deny this is the happiest I've ever seen him. It's like he's finally found his place in the world."

"I understand your concern about whether buying the winery was a good business move," Julian said thoughtfully. "But there's something to be said for finding your place in the world. And if anyone can help your father elevate the winery to its full potential, it's the Abbotts. Even Cole—who isn't involved in running the distillery—has proven himself to be a brilliant businessman."

Julian chuckled before continuing. "Cole shocked the entire town, including his family, when he didn't go into the family business. They thought he'd fail and come crawling back to the distillery. But going into construction and development was right for him. I think they all appreciate that now."

Chandra couldn't help feeling bad for her father, knowing now that he'd felt trapped in his adopted family's business all those years. She'd also felt stifled by Valentine Textiles. The sudden end of her engagement had given her the courage to walk away, and it was what she'd needed to do at the time. But she'd also distanced herself from most of her family. That she regretted. Spending the past few days with her father and siblings made that abundantly clear.

"Do you ever regret becoming a doctor?" Chandra asked.

"No." His answer was immediate. "True, I made the decision hoping it would be a magic bullet that would fix things between me and my mom. And the deal I made with Joe Abbott forced me to return home when I would've preferred to stay in Philly. But I love helping people. Being there for them in life-changing ways." He glanced over at her. "Sounds sappy, right?"

"Sappy with a side of flower child." They both laughed. "But I like it, and I like you. You're a genuinely good guy, Dr. Julian Brandon. Magnolia Lake is lucky to have you for the next four years. You were well worth the investment."

"Thanks." Julian covered her hand, perched on the console between them, with his own. She thought about when he'd offered her his hand on the plane. "And thank you for defusing things with my mother. She was hurt and probably embarrassed to learn about us from town gossip. You handled the situation brilliantly. I'm not surprised your father wants to make you the company CEO."

Her father, who was doing his best to talk them all into joining the company, had mentioned during dinner that he was offering her the role of CEO. She was flattered, but she couldn't accept the position.

Maybe her current company wasn't the perfect fit. But she'd worked hard toward her goal of joining the management team. She was too close to walk away now. If she did, what had the past five years been for?

She needed to prove she could succeed on her own. Not because her surname was on the company letterhead.

"I appreciate my dad's confidence in me," Chandra said. "But I'm so close to achieving a goal in my career. I'm not prepared to walk away."

"But are you happy?" Julian asked. "I only ask because the way you describe it…it sounds pretty rough."

"Not everyone gets to play the hero." Chandra realized she sounded defensive. "I honestly don't know a lot of people who'd say they love their job."

"True. But we spend so much time at work. Seems a shame to spend that much time doing something we don't actually enjoy." He shrugged. "But you obviously know what's best for you."

Do I?

Chandra looked out the window, unsure how to respond. She wanted to tell Julian he should mind his own business. After all, he'd been dragged back to Magnolia Lake to settle a debt with the Abbotts based on a commitment he'd made as a teen.

Who is he to be doling out life and career advice?

But a part of her recognized the truth in what he'd said.

Julian turned onto a paved road that ran through a wooded area. A few streetlights dotted the path as he turned down another road and a lake came into view. The gorgeous moon was reflected in the water.

"Julian, the sky here is absolutely stunning." Chandra craned her neck to take in the night sky. "The moon is so brilliant, and the stars are so vivid."

He parked the SUV. "You said you missed seeing the stars, and this is one of my favorite places in the world.

My dad brought me here to fish when I was a kid. Sometimes, we'd pitch a tent by the lake and spend the night looking at the constellations with this telescope he bought for my eighth birthday. So I thought you'd—"

Chandra kissed his cheek. "This is perfect, Julian. Can we take a stroll around the lake?"

Julian seemed stunned by her kiss. "I didn't think you'd want to walk in those." He indicated her silver stilettos.

She slipped them off and pulled a pair of foldable black Italian leather ballet flats from her bag. "These things are lifesavers."

They both stepped out of the SUV and Julian pulled a heather-gray coat from the back seat. He held it up. "The temperature has dropped quite a bit. Better put this on."

She removed the red shawl that provided little warmth against the chill of the crisp fall night air. Then she slipped her arms into the coat that carried Julian's clean, woodsy, masculine scent. She pulled the fabric around her. "Thank you. But what about you? You'll freeze out here."

"I'm fine." Julian buttoned his suit jacket.

Julian locked the vehicle and extended his hand. Chandra slipped her hand into his and they set off toward the well-lit path that circled the lake. A chilly breeze rustled her hair, the strands whipping across her face.

"What was your life like in Philadelphia?"

"Busy, but good. I worked the ER at a suburban hospital. Volunteered at a clinic in an underserved community. Did some real estate investing."

"You weren't kidding about being busy." She laughed. "What part of the city did you live in?"

"Phoenixville. It's a great little artsy neighborhood with tons of restaurants. I felt at home there."

"It sounds nice, but I'd be tempted to try a different restaurant every night."

"When I first moved to the area, a fellow resident and I shared an apartment above an Italian restaurant. We could smell everything they were cooking. We both gained about twenty pounds." He chuckled.

Chandra could relate. Her freshman fifteen had been more of a freshman twenty-five. Most of which was still with her.

"And how is it being back here and living a slower, quieter life?" she asked.

"I'm slowly adjusting to having my own practice and to being back home," he admitted. "And getting to know you has been a pleasant surprise." His dark eyes flickered. "But enough about me. What made you leave the family business and move to San Diego?"

"A broken engagement weeks before my wedding day." Chandra's cheeks heated with embarrassment. "I needed a change and to prove to myself that I could make it in a company my family didn't own. So I accepted a position in San Diego."

"The separation from your family must've been tough."

"It was. I cried nearly every day for the first few months. I thought about going back home a lot in the beginning. But I felt like I had something to prove. I'd just had a failed relationship. I didn't want to admit that I'd failed in my career, too."

"Sounds like a lot of pressure." Julian threaded his fingers through hers and squeezed her hand.

"It was. Nolan, Sebastian and Alonzo felt like I'd abandoned them, like our mother. I missed my brothers, but I was too proud to admit I wanted to come home. So I pulled away. Threw myself into my work, so I didn't have time to feel homesick or wonder why I hadn't been enough for my fiancé, who'd been hooking up with an ex."

After all this time, knowing she hadn't been enough for Edward still hurt. "The further I advanced at work, the less time I had to connect with my dad and siblings. I was the one who'd always kept everyone connected by planning family meals and holiday get-togethers. Once I stopped doing that, we started to drift apart."

She hadn't talked about this with anyone. Not even her family. But everything about being with Julian felt comfortable. Easy.

I can't let go of the sense that you and I were meant to meet.

Julian's words to her at the café echoed in her head.

Now who's being corny with a side of flower child?

They each had their roles in the family. The bohemian who believed in the wonders of the Universe was strictly Naya's territory. Chandra was the sensible one tasked with playing devil's advocate and raining on her dad's and siblings' parades with a healthy dose of reality. She wasn't the one who chased sunshine and rainbows and believed everything would work out. In her experience, it rarely did.

They sat on a covered bench overlooking the lake.

"This is the perfect spot." Julian gestured toward the star-filled sky.

He'd pointed out various constellations as they'd walked the trail around the lake. But this was the best vantage point from which to study the moon and all of the stars.

"The moon is beautiful tonight," Chandra marveled. A deep sense of contentment washed over her.

"It's a waning gibbous moon, which follows the full moon. About seventy-five percent of it is illuminated by the sun tonight. Those dark splotches you see are large plains of basaltic rock caused by volcanic activity nearly four billion years ago. And the craters…" Julian glanced over at her, then dragged a hand down his face. "Sorry. I'm boring you to tears."

"No, you aren't." Chandra smiled. "This is fascinating. And so are you, Julian. Thank you for bringing me here. This place is obviously very special to you. It means a lot that you wanted to share it with me. It's the perfect end to our night."

Julian stared at her; his dark eyes filled with heat. "What if we didn't want our night to end just yet?"

"What did you have in mind, Dr. Brandon? Though I should warn you that I'm not the kind of girl who makes out in the woods…especially on a first date."

Julian chuckled, leaning in closer. His breath, visible in the chilly night air, warmed her face. "Fair. But this isn't our first date. It's our fifth."

"Is this about that hand-holding thing again?" She studied his handsome features beneath the moonlight.

"Hey, don't knock it." Julian's dark eyes glittered with amusement. But there was heat in them, too. "And since lunch at the café was our third date, you kissed me under the mistletoe on our fourth date. That makes this our fifth date."

Didn't quite hit her six-date rule...but close enough.

"Hmm..." She tried to hold back a grin. "Keep talking."

"And while I don't intend to make out with you in the woods—" he tipped her chin, his gaze locked with hers "—I would like very much to kiss you beneath the waning gibbous moon."

Julian captured her lips in a kiss as he cradled her cheek.

Chandra's eyes drifted closed as she sank into the lusciousness of Julian's kiss, his full lips pressed to hers. His large hand cradling her cheek.

Their earlier kiss had been good but tame compared to this. Here beneath the beautiful night sky, and away from prying eyes, Julian's kiss was hungry and eager. Her response needy and desperate. The intensity of the kiss growing with each moment beneath the stars.

Julian's tongue teased the seam of her lips, then slipped between them and glided against hers. Chandra relished the taste of apple crumb pie and the hints of the Zinfandel wine, supplied by her family's new winery. Julian slid his fingers into the nape of her hair as his thumbs grazed her cheeks.

Chandra sighed softly, leaning into him. Needing more contact with the hard body that had teased her earlier when they'd slow danced.

Julian's tongue ravished her mouth, the sensation filling her body with heat. Her nipples pebbled, and the space between her thighs grew damp and ached for his touch.

"So is this why you really brought me here?" she teased, when he finally broke their kiss. "To play doctor in the woods?"

Julian chuckled, those penetrating dark eyes glittering in the moonlight. "I really wanted you to see how incredible the night sky is here." He gazed reverently at the sky above them before meeting her eyes again. "But if you're asking if I'd hoped for another chance to kiss you—for real this time—the answer to that is an unapologetic *hell yes*."

Chandra nibbled on her lower lip, all of the reasons she shouldn't do this cycling through her brain.

Julian was too young for her. Even if he wasn't, she'd be leaving soon, negating the possibility of anything serious between them. And something purely casual could get messy. If she agreed to a one-night stand, they'd undoubtedly cross paths whenever she visited her dad. Which could be…awkward.

Chandra frowned, slowly pulling away. She could see the disappointment on Julian's handsome face. He knew she was going to say no. Which was the sensible choice. And wasn't that her role? The sensible, play-it-safe oldest daughter and surrogate mother to her siblings?

But are you happy?

Julian's earlier words echoed in her head. She sighed. Her father hadn't played it safe when he'd purchased the vineyard once owned by his biological mother's family. And look how much happier he was.

She wasn't expecting anything from Julian. But maybe she could permit herself the euphoria she felt whenever she was with him. Because it'd been more than five years since anyone had made her feel this way.

Didn't she at least deserve temporary bliss?

Chandra swallowed hard, her heart racing. "I assume we're going to your place. Mine isn't an option."

Julian's eyes widened with surprise. "Got the perfect spot in mind."

He gave her a quick kiss, then took her hand, before leading her back to his SUV. He took the road in the opposite direction from which they'd come. Up the road just a bit, he pulled into the driveway of an idyllic little cabin with a large front porch.

"This is your place?" Chandra slapped his arm, playfully.

"The cabin is part of the package, too."

"You brought me to stargaze at a spot that just happens to be about five feet from your bedroom, huh? Very crafty, Dr. Jules." Chandra shook a finger at him. "You'd better be glad you're a *really* good kisser."

"Noted." Julian winked.

The cabin was far more luxurious on the inside than its rustic outer appearance suggested. The decor was warm and modern, accented by lots of dark leather and warm, natural woods. Folding glass doors led to a well-lit patio out back.

"The cabin…it's really nice." Now that they were there, Chandra's stomach was doing somersaults. And she was sure Julian could hear the thud of her heartbeat.

This was why she'd essentially given up on dating. She wasn't good at dealing with the unfamiliar. Not knowing a potential lover's wants, expectations or predilections.

Would he be awful in bed? Would he ask her to do

something that made her uncomfortable? When was the last time he'd vacuumed his room or changed his sheets?

Chandra heaved a quiet sigh, her eyes drifting closed. Suddenly, Julian was standing in front of her. One hand was planted on her hip; the other cupped her chin.

"Chandra, it's okay." His tone was reassuring, and a genuine smile lit his eyes. "We'll take this as fast or as slow as you'd like. If all you want to do is sit on that sofa and watch episodes of *Orphan Black* with me, then that's what we'll do." He dropped a soft kiss on her lips. "No pressure, all right?"

She nodded and her pulse slowed a little. "Are you always this sweet and considerate?" she asked. "I'm beginning to think you can't be real."

"I've been a selfish jerk plenty of times in my life. Hopefully, I'm a better person now."

"Undoubtedly." Chandra smoothed her hands down the lapels of the suit that hugged his athletic body so well.

"Can I get you a drink or maybe a snack?" Julian offered.

Chandra studied Julian's face and tried to summon a little of Naya's "I know what I want, and I'm not afraid to ask for it" courage.

"The only snack I'm interested in tonight is you." Chandra laughed when Julian's eyes darkened, and he licked his lower lip. "But first, can I use your restroom?"

"Absolutely." He held up a finger. "Just give me a sec."

Julian disappeared down a hallway, returning a minute or two later. Then he showed her the bathroom off the main bedroom.

Chandra stepped inside the restroom and closed the door, her back pressed to the wall.

Last chance to chicken out.

Eleven

Julian opened a bottle of his favorite red Moscato and filled two glasses halfway. When he returned to his bedroom, Chandra was emerging from the bathroom. She stood still, as if frozen in place.

"Wine?" He lifted a glass.

"Please." Chandra dropped her handbag on the dresser and accepted the glass of wine.

She took a healthy sip, then sucked in a deep breath. She was reluctant at the least—terrified at worst.

Julian had dreamed of having Chandra Valentine in his bed since the day they'd met. But the night of mind-blowing pleasure he'd envisioned couldn't happen if she was as skittish as a cornered rabbit. He wanted them both to remember this night fondly.

So a literal Netflix and Chill night it would be.

"Why don't I give you the penny tour?" he asked. A

subtle attempt to get them out of the bedroom, so she'd be more comfortable.

Chandra set down her glass roughly and stalked toward him, her eyes filled with heat. She ran her palms down his navy shirt. "Later?"

"You're sure? Because as much as I want this…I need you to know there's absolutely no press—"

Chandra's mouth was suddenly on his, her fingers pressed to his back.

Julian set down his glass of wine, too. He kissed her, eager to taste her mouth again. His hands glided down over her firm, round bottom as he tugged her against him, his hardened length pinned between them.

Chandra tugged his shirt from the waist of his pants and fumbled with the buttons, her hands trembling slightly. As the kiss escalated, they undressed each other with a growing sense of urgency. One garment after another drifted to the floor between frantic kisses. Finally, bare bodies pressed together, they tumbled into his bed and climbed beneath the covers. Julian trailed kisses down her neck and chest, his tongue teasing one of the beaded tips.

She arched into his touch, a soft murmur emanating from her lips. He'd wanted to taste every inch of her soft brown skin. To know what sounds she'd make as he swirled his tongue around her dark brown nipples. Had wondered how Chandra would react when he feasted on her—and he couldn't wait any longer to find out.

Julian kissed his way down her body. Over her soft rounded belly, which tensed as he sank lower. Over the neat tract of dark curls at the apex of the thick thighs that had teased him all night.

He pressed a kiss to the glistening swollen flesh

between her thighs. Then another and another. Julian spread her with his thumbs, loving the shallow breaths and increasingly desperate murmurs each swipe of his tongue elicited.

Chandra moaned, her hips undulating and her fingers spiking into his hair as she rode his tongue until she shattered. Her body tensed and she dug her heels into the mattress as she muttered his name again and again.

As beautiful as Chandra was on any given day, she was even more beautiful sated. Her dewy skin glowed. Her chest rose and fell with each shallow breath.

If he got to see Chandra fall apart like that every day for the rest of his life, he'd never tire of it. Julian kissed the junction of her neck and shoulder.

Chandra's bashful smile made her even more beautiful.

"God, I love that smile." Julian stroked her cheek and her smile deepened.

"Do that again and I guarantee you'll see a lot more of it." Chandra flashed him a wicked grin as she stroked his stubbled chin.

Julian's tongue glided along his lower lip, salty with the taste of her, and he winked. "Is that a personal challenge? Because from the moment I saw you in those sparkly stilettos tonight, I've been imagining them dangling over my shoulders with my mouth on that—"

"You, Dr. Brandon, have a filthy mind and a deliciously dirty mouth." Her hands trailed up his chest. "And I'm definitely here for it."

He devoured her mouth with a hungry kiss as her hands moved down his back, her fingernails grazing his skin. Julian reached inside the nightstand and tore into the box of condoms. He ripped open a packet and sheathed himself.

He savored the sensation as he inched inside her, loving how snugly her body enveloped his. As if they were two pieces designed to fit together.

Chandra's lips parted on a soft gasp once he was fully seated, and he captured her mouth in a kiss. He moved his hips slowly, determined to appreciate every single moment of this. But as with every taste of her sweet lips, every delicious sensation of pleasure that rolled up his spine only made him desperate for more of her.

When he lifted her leg over his shoulder and ground his hips against hers, Chandra's murmurs turned to soft moans, then insistent pleas. Finally, she called his name, her muscles tensing and her back arching. Her inner walls clenched his heated flesh, pulling him in deeper as she reached her climax.

He kissed her hard, swallowing her cries. Her nails dug into his skin, as if she was marking him as hers. His hips moved until he, too, tumbled over the edge, Chandra's name on his lips. Julian heaved a sigh and collapsed onto the bed beside her. He gathered her in his arms, their labored breathing the only sounds in the room.

Julian kissed Chandra's temple. "Meeting you is the absolute best thing that's happened since I returned to town."

"We're supposed to say that seeing our families is the best thing that's happened since we've been here." Chandra grazed his nipple with her thumb and dropped a kiss on his chest. "But just between us...same."

Chandra was funny, smart and beautiful. He'd loved

every moment he'd spent getting to know her. But he wanted to know more—everything there was to know about Chandra Valentine. Her history. Her hopes for the future. What she liked for breakfast. And all of the ways she liked to be pleased.

Chandra would return to San Diego in a week. A week with this amazing woman could never be enough. But if it was all he had, he'd enjoy every moment he got to spend with this goddess who made his spine tingle and his heart skip a beat.

Julian's eyes fluttered open to the sound of water running in the bathroom. Chandra stepped into the darkened bedroom fully dressed. She sifted her fingers through her disheveled hair.

He propped himself up on one elbow and rubbed the sleep from his eyes. "You're leaving? I was hoping to impress you with my breakfast skills."

"You cook?" Chandra arched an eyebrow.

"My repertoire is limited, but the things I do cook are damn good. Like my variations on French toast."

"Such as?" Her interest was piqued, giving him the slightest hope that she'd crawl her fine ass back into bed with him.

"Crème brûlée French toast, churro French toast, banana bread French toast…"

"You're a regular French toast connoisseur, aren't you?" Her kiss-swollen lips, bearing only a hint of her lip gloss, formed a reluctant smile that tugged at something in his chest. "Would've figured you for a bacon guy."

She wasn't wrong. He had six pounds of bacon in his

freezer. But she didn't need to know she'd read him right. *Again.*

"If you stay, I might surprise you in a few more ways." He grabbed her hand, tugging her closer.

"I didn't think you'd want me to stay. I mean, I assumed this was just—"

"A one-night stand?"

"Well, yes." She shrugged. "I'll be gone in a week."

"Then we should make the most of that time." He pulled her onto his lap, peppering her neck and shoulder with kisses.

Chandra made a purring sound that vibrated in his chest. He fought the urge to strip her naked and take her again. Remind her that he was a grown-ass man whose stroke game and tongue skills were on point, given how fervently she'd called his name each time he'd taken her over the edge.

"As tempting as that sounds, I really do need to get back. I came here to check on my dad and spend time with my siblings. It would be rude if I spent my entire vacation banging the town's baby doctor." She gave him a teasing smile, followed by a quick kiss. Then she retrieved her ballet flats and sat at the foot of the bed to put them on.

"Fair point." Julian groaned. "I'll drive you over to the winery."

"I'll call a car service."

"Sweetheart, this is Magnolia Lake, not San Diego. There won't be any car service available at—" he glanced at his watch "—one forty a.m."

"Right." Chandra furrowed her brows, and her mouth

twisted as she assessed the situation, which only made her more adorable. "Then I'll just call my—"

"Chandra, I brought you here. And I'm going to deliver you home safe and sound. Just like I promised your dad." He got out of bed and pulled on his boxers.

"Thank you." The smile she flashed was almost shy. He could swear his heart did a somersault in his chest.

What the hell is this woman doing to me?

If he had good sense, he'd drop Chandra at home, thank her for a wonderful evening and wish her safe travels without any intentions of seeing her again. She didn't want to get serious, and the complications of a relationship that would tie him to Magnolia Lake were the last thing he needed.

But apparently, he lacked a sense of self-preservation.

When he pulled into the driveway of the old winery and turned off his engine, he kissed Chandra goodnight. But the kiss didn't feel like a goodbye.

"I realize you came here to spend time with your family," he whispered between kisses to her full, lush lips. "And that you'll only be here a few more days. But I'd really like to see you again before you leave, Chandra."

Chandra nibbled on her lower lip, then nodded. She pressed a final kiss to his lips. "I'll try."

Julian got out and opened the door for Chandra. Her fancy heels were hooked over the strap of her purse.

"I'll walk you to the door."

"That isn't necessary. I texted Naya. She left the back light on and the door unlocked."

Julian forced a smile to mask his disappointment that their evening was officially at an end. "Then text me to let me know you got inside safe. Here…" He held out his hand.

When Chandra unlocked her phone and handed it to him, he scrolled to her contacts, added his cell phone number, then typed in his information. Julian handed the phone back.

"Text me once you're inside safe and sound, or I *will* knock on that door to make sure you're all right."

"I don't doubt it." Chandra slipped the phone into her bag.

"I look forward to seeing you again." He kissed her.

"Good night, Dr. Brandon."

"Good night, Ms. Valentine." Julian sighed quietly as he watched Chandra strut toward the back door of the winery.

He climbed back into his SUV and waited patiently until a message appeared on his phone.

I'm inside. Thank you for a lovely night under the waning gibbous moon.

He added her number to his contacts, then turned around and pulled out of the drive.

Maybe neither of them was looking for a relationship. But perhaps they'd stumbled into one just the same.

Twelve

A smile spread across Chandra's face when she reviewed the contact information Julian had typed into her phone.

Julian "Baby Doctor" Brandon.

The man had a self-deprecating sense of humor that made him even more adorable. It was a refreshing change from the pompous, self-important assholes she was accustomed to dealing with.

Chandra was about to tiptoe up to bed, but there was a slamming sound, followed by a woot and raucous laughter.

She followed the voices to the game room.

"Hey there, sis. So… How was your night?" Naya asked in a singsong voice as she Groucho Marxed her perfectly arched eyebrows up and down.

"Don't answer that." Sebastian held up a hand. "I don't think any of us *really* want to hear the answer."

Her father and brothers agreed.

"Speak for yourselves. I want *all* the tea. The dirtier, the better." Her sister giggled. "You can tell me all about Dr. Brandon's *bedside manner* later." She winked.

"You're a mess." Chandra poked her sister's arm.

The room settled into an uncomfortable silence.

Chandra didn't miss this part of not being around her father and brothers as much anymore. She was a grown woman. Yet she felt like a teenager who'd been busted making out in a parked car with her boyfriend.

"What are you all still doing up? Please tell me you weren't waiting up for me," Chandra said.

"Not me," Nyles offered quickly. "Me and my partner here are whipping that collective ass." He tipped his chin toward Alonzo, who responded with a cocky grin and a head nod. "We're playing rise and fly Bid Whist and none of these chumps have been able to unseat us all night."

"That baby brother of yours has been talking shit for the past two hours." Her father went to the sideboard and poured himself a glass of King's Finest Bourbon and added a splash of soda. "I want someone else to win just to shut him up."

Chandra couldn't help thinking how surreal it was that her father had been drinking King's Finest Bourbon for decades, not realizing the company was owned by his half brother.

"He wasn't talking that mess when you and I ran through the lot of them a few years ago." Her father flashed a warm smile at Chandra and draped an arm over her shoulder.

The memory elicited a smile. It was the last time

they'd all been together like this before coming to Magnolia Lake. After spending the past few days with her family, she realized how much she missed them. Even trash-talking Nyles.

Chandra leaned her head on her dad's shoulder. He didn't seem quite as tall as he once had. "Good memories."

They watched Alonzo and Nyles, who were well on their way to running a Boston on Nolan and Sebastian.

"Everything good, kiddo?" Her father's brows knitted with concern.

"Of course." Chandra ran her fingers through her hair, wondering if it looked like she'd just tumbled out of bed with the hot young doctor. "I'm an adult, Dad. And sometimes I do *adult* things."

"I realize that, sweetheart, and I'm not arguing. I just want to make sure my baby girl is okay. Been worried about you since you called off your engagement and took off for San Diego."

"That's a generous way to put it, Dad." Her father knew very well that Edward had been the one who'd ended things, taking her completely by surprise. She'd been foolish enough to think they were happy. Despite the signs that indicated otherwise. "Besides, I'm thirty-nine. I'd think you'd be over worrying about me."

"Never. You will *always* be my baby girl. I can still remember the first time I held you in my arms. And the way you used to love it when I lifted you onto my shoulders and trotted through our backyard. Those memories will always live here." He tapped the half-empty glass against his chest. "And worrying about your kids… that's something a parent does till the day they die."

"Maybe that's what *good* parents do." Chandra's eyes stung.

Her mother had walked away more than thirty years ago. Her stepmother—Nyles and Naya's mother—had walked away when the twins were just three years old. Chandra should be over the pain and anger of both women—whom she'd loved and adored—abandoning them. So why did discussing her mother's leaving still feel like a crushing weight on her chest?

"Not everyone is cut out to be a parent, sweetheart. Problem is, most folks don't figure that out until they actually have children." Her father drained the remainder of his bourbon, then turned to her. "I'm under no illusion that I was father-of-the-year material. But I loved you kids…and your mothers."

"So you weren't perfect. Who is?" Chandra shrugged. "But you were there for us then, and you're here for us now. We appreciate everything you've done and everything you're trying to do."

Her father's face brightened, and he pulled her into a bear hug. "I just need to know you're safe and that you're happy. That's all I want for all of you."

"That's what we want for you, too, Dad. So if buying this place and building your own empire is what makes you happy, I'll do whatever I can to support that. But I just can't—"

"I understand." He gave her a pained smile. "But the dream isn't just building an empire, sweetheart. It's building it *together.* With all of you by my side. I know you can't see my vision yet. But I'm not giving up." He winked.

"Well, I'm exhausted," Chandra said.

"I'll bet you are," Naya chimed in, her mouth twisted in a mischievous grin.

Chandra narrowed her gaze at her younger sister in a silent *behave*. A look Chandra had honed when she was young and had often been left in charge of her younger siblings.

Naya giggled, undaunted, and munched on a handful of tortilla chips.

"I'm going to bed. We've got a lot to do around here before I return to San Diego." Chandra kissed her father on the cheek and bade her siblings good-night. Then she showered and got ready for bed. But she tossed and turned, unable to fall asleep. She couldn't stop thinking about the amazing night she'd had with Julian and how much she liked him.

Her skin tingled as her mind replayed the visceral memory of how Julian had trailed kisses over her skin.

The sex had been phenomenal. But there was so much more to Dr. Julian Brandon.

He was caring and insightful. He'd known just what to say to calm and reassure her. He'd swooped in and extracted her from her car, turned over in that ditch, like a modern-day knight in shining armor. She hadn't been able to stop thinking about him long before she'd encountered him in that doctor's office.

Chandra couldn't deny that she really, *really* liked Julian. But the young doctor was an indulgence Chandra couldn't afford.

He didn't fit into her plan for a big promotion and a corner office back in San Diego. And the past few days had reminded her she needed to be a more engaged daughter and a better sister. Because despite what they all claimed, it was obvious that the kids *weren't* all right. Something was going on with each and every one of them, and as the family fixer, she couldn't let that go. So she didn't have time for a relationship with the pretty-boy, small-town doctor who lived two thousand miles from the place she called home.

Still, she couldn't help smiling whenever she thought about Julian. And she hadn't laughed this much in years.

A relationship was out of the question. But perhaps a tension-relieving, no-strings fling before she returned to the stress of her real life was *exactly* what the doctor ordered.

Thirteen

Julian strolled out of the King's Finest Family Restaurant with Chandra's hand tucked firmly in his. He was grinning like an idiot, but he couldn't care less. He was beyond happy.

He and Chandra had managed to spend time together nearly every day for the past week. Julian had been pleasantly surprised when she'd called him the day after the Abbotts' party to say she'd love to see the lake in the daytime.

They'd taken a lunchtime stroll around the lake, then spent the afternoon in his bed before going their separate ways and having dinner with their families. And since then, he and Chandra had eaten lunch together at the café every day at one. On Tuesday and Thursday evenings, she'd ditched movie or game nights with her family, spending those evenings with him before returning to the winery later.

The more time they spent together, the more he realized that Chandra was someone he could imagine a future with. But their time together was running out. The next day she would board a plane to San Diego. It was a reality Julian had been trying his damnedest not to dwell on.

"Is everything okay?" Chandra had stopped walking. "You're a million miles away. You nearly walked past your office."

He turned toward the redbrick building bearing the Abbott family's name. The medical building was only a few doors from the restaurant, so they'd parked in his reserved spot there and walked down. During dinner, he'd gotten a call from a patient. He needed to call in a new prescription for Mrs. Donaldson. But before calling in an alternate medication, he wanted to double-check the list of blood pressure medicines Doc Johnson had already tried and review the notes of her reaction to each.

"Sorry I'm a little distracted. I was running through the list of meds I might try with this patient. Let me get this prescription sorted out. Then you'll have my complete focus." He kissed her. "Promise."

They went up to his office and he logged on to his computer, while Chandra wandered the space. After he'd hung up with the pharmacy, she appeared in the doorway of his office. Her eyes glittered with mischief.

"Picture this..." Chandra held up her hands, as if she was framing him in a camera lens. "Me on an exam table with my feet in stirrups and you seated on that little red stool of yours." She laughed when his eyes went wide. "You asked about sexual fantasies." She shrugged. "This one just came to me."

"I will never, ever, be able to get the image of me feasting on you while you're spread out on an exam table out of my head." Julian adjusted himself before sitting on the front edge of the desk. "But truthfully, I have to conduct some pretty gross procedures in those exam rooms. So they're the least sexy places in the world to me."

"And now I'll never get *that* out of my head." Chandra frowned. "That just killed the fantasy."

Julian grasped Chandra's uninjured wrist and tugged her closer. "Or maybe we modify the fantasy. Like you seated on the edge of my desk instead. Or…" He closed his eyes, shuddering at the thought that entered his head.

"Or?" Chandra studied his face.

"I have the sudden urge to bend you over this desk and take you from behind." His voice was gruff, and a flash of heat crawled up his neck.

Chandra's smile widened. "I'll take what's behind Door #2, please." She locked the door, then stood between his open legs as he sat on the edge of his desk. He couldn't help marveling over how beautiful she was.

He captured her lips in a kiss, his arms encircling her waist. Julian molded Chandra's tempting curves against his body, aching to be buried inside her. Everything about this woman fueled his unquenchable desire for her.

The following afternoon she'd head back to San Diego, and they'd part ways as friends. He'd agreed to that, because it was all Chandra wanted. But the truth was *he* wanted more of her kiss. More of her touch.

More time getting lost in those gorgeous brown eyes as they talked and laughed together.

His hands glided over her firm bottom as he tugged Chandra closer, their hunger for one another increasingly obvious.

Julian glided a hand up her outer thigh, beneath the flouncy little black skirt, as he devoured her mouth with a greedy kiss, relishing the sweet taste of her full lips.

"Please tell me you have a condom," she whispered against his lips.

He didn't carry any in his wallet, but he kept some in a bowl by the door for patients who needed them but were too embarrassed to ask. It was a tradition Doc Johnson had established two decades ago. Controversial at the time. But the Abbotts had backed Doc Johnson, and eventually, many of his loudest opposers grudgingly came to accept the wisdom of it.

"By the door." He trailed kisses down her neck.

Chandra glanced over her shoulder. "Those are… *colorful.*"

Not his usual brand or size, but they'd do in a pinch.

Chandra sifted through the bowl filled with prophylactics in a range of rainbow colors. She picked a purple one and sashayed toward him, a smirk curving her sensuous lips.

He kissed her, his tongue gliding along hers as he palmed her full breast and grazed its pebbled tip with his thumb.

Chandra fumbled with his belt, unfastening it and then unzipping his jeans. She slipped her hand beneath the waistband of his boxers, her palm gliding along his fevered flesh as she stroked him with a loose grip.

Then she tightened her grip and fisted him with a steady stroke.

"Fuck," he muttered against her lips.

Julian could barely think. Hell, he could barely breathe. His brain was capable of processing only two thoughts. One: he wanted to be buried so deeply inside Chandra that it would feel as if they were a single being. Two: he needed more moments like this with her.

Julian leaned into the first thought—the one over which he had control. He pushed the second thought from his head.

"Condom. On," he whispered roughly, his pulse racing.

It took three tries, but she ripped open the packet. She managed to inch the glaringly purple condom down his length, despite the snug fit.

"That seems...*uncomfortable*." Chandra frowned. "Maybe we should wait until we get back to your place."

Julian skimmed his palm up the inside of Chandra's thigh and tugged aside the soaked panel of lace. She gasped softly when he glided his fingers back and forth over her sex.

"I'm willing to power through it, if you are," he murmured between kisses to her throat. He could barely hold back a smirk as she sighed softly, her hips moving against his hand as she gripped his shoulders and whispered *yes* again and again.

Julian plunged two fingers inside her, his thumb massaging the tight bundle of nerves. He swallowed her quiet gasp, his tongue searching hers as he slipped his fingers inside her, then retracted them, again and again, her legs wobbling. Chandra rode his hand until her body went stiff and she cried out his name so loudly he was glad no one else was working in the building on a Saturday afternoon.

In one swift move, he stood behind Chandra and lifted her skirt. He yanked the soaked fabric of her panties aside and slid into her. The sensation sent a shudder up his spine.

"Fuck, you feel incredible, Chandra." He kissed her neck and shoulder as he palmed her breast, teasing the tip with his thumb. His other hand braced her hip as he thrust into her from behind.

The sounds of their heavy breathing, his determined grunts, her quiet groans and their bodies meeting again and again filled the quiet office. Like an erotic symphony. The honeysuckle scent of her perfume mingled in the air with the scent of her arousal—a scent and taste he knew well.

Julian released her breast, now exposed by her disheveled blouse. He tipped Chandra's chin, drinking in the intoxicating expression on her gorgeous face. Julian captured her lips with his own, his tongue exploring the cavern of her mouth.

He pulled his hand from her hip and stroked her clit as he moved inside her, bringing her closer to the edge. Chandra flew apart, her body trembling as she whimpered his name. Julian kissed her neck, then her shoulder. His hips moving faster, urged on by the pulsing of her walls around his painfully hardened shaft. His body stiffened and his head felt light with the orgasm that seemed to slam into his chest, stealing his breath.

His heart raced as he quietly cursed and moaned, her name on his lips.

The sounds of their shallow breathing seemed to

echo off the walls of the quiet space. But despite the euphoria of the moment, Julian couldn't help feeling a deep, aching sense of loss looming.

He'd fallen hard for Chandra. But tomorrow, she'd be gone.

Julian buried his face in Chandra's neck, inhaling the subtle scent he'd come to crave: a mingling of her honeysuckle perfume and the sweet coconut-and-vanilla scent of her dark hair. He kissed the shell of her ear.

"Don't go, Chandra," he whispered, then pressed another kiss to her ear. "Not yet. Please."

Chandra turned over her shoulder, her brown eyes glistening with unshed tears. She pressed her lips into a smile and cradled his cheek. "I wish we had more time, Julian. But we'd only be delaying the inevitable."

He'd known her answer before the plea had left his mouth. But he couldn't let her walk away without begging her to stay.

Julian nodded, then kissed her shoulder, their bodies still connected. "Of course. Let me take care of this. Then we can head out of here."

Before he could pull away completely, Chandra hooked an arm around him. "I have to return to work, but I could work remotely this week and head back to California next week. After that, if you're ever in San Diego and we're both free…"

"I'd really like that." Julian lifted Chandra's chin and she twisted her body, meeting his lips in a soft, warm kiss that set his heart and his body on fire.

Julian didn't know what would happen with them beyond next week. But he was glad he wasn't the only one who wasn't ready for this to end.

Fourteen

One Month Later

Chandra found a spot in the parking garage of the building that housed Phillips Athletic Wear. While she waited in the lobby for the elevator, she fired off a group text message to her sister, Naya, and her brother Alonzo. They'd spent the past few days brainstorming event ideas for the winery in a text message chain.

Only Naya and Nolan had accepted their father's invitation to join the winery. Naya was Valentine Vineyards' PR & events coordinator. Nolan would formally assume the role of CFO of Valentine Vineyards once he was done facilitating the sale of the textile firm.

But while Chandra, Sebastian, Alonzo and Nyles had declined to join the newly acquired family firm, they'd all been regularly consulted by their father, Nolan and

Naya as they made plans for the official launch of the newly rebranded winery. During their time in Magnolia Lake, she, her dad and her siblings had worked with a graphic designer Max's wife, Quinn, had recommended. The woman created dynamic new branding for Valentine Vineyards, based on all of their input, including a logo, wine labels and signage.

It was exciting to be a part of shaping the new company from the start. In some ways, she envied Naya and Nolan being at the center of this exciting new family venture. But she'd been on a five-year-long mission, and she wouldn't let herself get derailed now. Not by her father's identity crisis, the discovery of mystery relatives or a sweet, handsome and far-too-young doctor who'd swept her off her feet.

Chandra stepped onto the elevator and punched the button for her floor. She scrolled through her phone, searching for Julian's latest text message.

Hey, beautiful. Hope you're doing well. Life around here just isn't the same without you. Miss you like crazy.

Chandra's heart fluttered. She could practically hear the words being uttered in Julian's deep, gravelly voice. His mouth pulled into a sexy grin that sent electricity down her spine.

She missed him, too. More than she could've imagined.

So much had changed since she'd boarded that plane to Magnolia Lake several weeks ago. She'd reconnected with her father and siblings, gotten to know her unknown relatives whom she really liked, discovered the beauty of the Smoky Mountains and the appeal of small-town living.

And she'd met, been rescued by, fake dated and screwed the brains out of the handsome young doctor.

Chandra couldn't stop thinking about Julian. They'd only met a couple of months ago. Yet the man had managed to turn her world upside down.

She'd finally met a man who seemed perfect. But in the cosmic joke that was her life, he was nearly a decade younger and lived two thousand miles away.

Julian was unbothered by their age difference. But Chandra couldn't help worrying what other people would think. Besides, did she honestly want to spend the next four years dating someone she'd get to see maybe one weekend a month?

"Good morning, Ms. Valentine." The distressed look on the face of Evelyn Santos, assistant to Chandra's boss Ethan, caused uneasiness to creep up her spine.

Ethan and Evelyn were based in Nashville. What were they doing in San Diego unannounced?

"Good morning, Evelyn. I didn't realize Ethan was in town."

"Something came up. Ethan and Elliot are in the conference room waiting for you." Evelyn's eyes didn't meet Chandra's.

The uneasiness in her gut ratcheted up a notch. She was hit by a wave of nausea.

The Phillips brothers co-owned the firm. Ethan, the CEO based in Nashville, had hired her five years ago. She'd been sent to San Diego to turn things around and essentially babysit Elliot Phillips, whose title as COO was more of a wish than a job description.

For the past five years, she'd effectively been running the firm's San Diego operations. And while Elliot resented that his brother had sent her there, he seemed content to allow her to do the actual work while he took credit for it with board members and the media. Chandra had endured it because Elliot intended to retire next year, and she'd be the logical choice for his replacement.

The apprehension she felt was a heightened version of the unsettling feeling she'd had since her return one month ago.

Elliot Phillips's resentment was evident in the dead-eyed smile he gave her each day. But since her return, his grin was different. Like he knew something she didn't.

"Let me stop at my office and—"

"Actually, Ethan asked that I bring you *straight* to the conference room." Evelyn's voice dripped with apology and her gaze landed somewhere over Chandra's left shoulder.

Chandra opened her mouth to demand to know what was going on, but Evelyn, whom she'd always liked, was simply doing her job. Chandra would take this up with Elliot and Ethan instead.

She stalked toward the glass conference room where the brothers were engaged in an argument, both of their faces red. She was undoubtedly the subject of their heated discussion.

Chandra shoved the glass door open. Both men stopped speaking and gave each other one last defiant look before turning to her.

"Good morning, Chandra. How was your trip to Seattle?" Ethan sounded exhausted. His usually bright blue eyes were dim.

"Productive, as always." Chandra set her bags on the table. "In fact, I was hoping to talk to you today about possible tech updates. But that clearly isn't what you're here to discuss."

She glared at Elliot, who had yet to speak and who looked like a cat who'd just had a bowl of cream with a hit of vodka and coffee liqueur. The man grinned, his dark eyes sparkling with malice.

"No, I'm afraid it isn't—" Ethan was saying.

"Come now, you act like this is a funeral or something." Elliot cut his brother off. "It isn't. This is good news, and a reason to celebrate."

"And why is that, Elliot?" The wave of nausea returned as Chandra anticipated his next words.

"My son has finally decided to join the firm." Elliot beamed like a proud father whose little boy had just nailed his piano recital.

"That's wonderful," Chandra said, not meaning it.

Nothing she knew about Elliot Phillips Jr. made her think he'd be an asset to the firm. But that hadn't impacted Elliot Sr.'s tenure, had it? Having the surname on the letterhead had been his only necessary qualification.

A knot tightened in Chandra's gut. "What role will he be taking on at the company?"

Elliot's grin deepened and his dark eyes narrowed. "He'll take on my role—once I retire, of course. But for now, he'll take on a newly minted role—executive vice president of supply chain, logistics and workplace."

Chandra's throat went dry and she swallowed hard

against the bile churning in her gut. Her fingernails dug into the palms of her hands, balled into trembling fists.

"You're firing me?"

"Of course not." Ethan's earnest tone was a deep contrast to his brother's amused grin. "Your work here has been stellar. Only a fool would let go of someone as brilliant as you."

"Then I'm being demoted?" She focused on Ethan but couldn't miss his brother's self-satisfied expression.

"Chandra, you're being a tad dramatic." Elliot sounded bored with the entire discussion. "You're the director of supply chain, logistics and workplace. Your role is unchanged. You'll simply report to EJ now instead of me." He shrugged. "It's all really quite simple." Elliot climbed to his feet and buttoned his tailored navy blue suit jacket. "Now, if you'll both excuse me, I have a meeting to attend."

Elliot strolled toward the door, then turned toward her with a sly grin. "Oh, by the way. There is *one* other change. Elliot Junior will be second in command now. His office space should reflect as much."

"You're giving your...*him*...my office?" Chandra tried her best not to let Elliot see just how infuriated she was.

"I had the movers make the switch over the weekend." Elliot's grin deepened. "Don't worry. Your things are all there and accounted for. Ms. Santos will show you to your new office. Welcome back, Ms. Valentine."

Chandra's cheeks and forehead were hot, her heart pounded in her chest and the sound of rushing blood filled her ears.

She could barely make out what Ethan was saying

as he rushed to speak. "I can only imagine how disappointed you must be right now, Chandra. Please know I did *everything* in my power to block this move."

"Then why is Junior sitting in my office, the heir apparent to a title you'd all but promised *me*?"

Ethan flinched but didn't back down. "Because in the end, this is a family-run firm. My family voted to keep it that way. Even if it isn't in the best interest of the company." Ethan pressed a hand to his forehead. Chandra knew enough about the man to realize he was genuinely perturbed. "I'm sorry, Chandra. I honestly didn't see this coming. I would never have led you to believe you'd be appointed as our next COO if I hadn't believed it possible."

"So now what, Ethan?" Chandra studied him. "Am I supposed to babysit Elliot Senior *and* Junior for the rest of my career?"

"You are the backbone of this place. The increased profitability we've experienced these past few years… you deserve all of the credit for it," Ethan conceded. "So I'm asking you to keep making this company better and more profitable. Like Elliot said, your position here is unchanged."

"I didn't come here for this, Ethan," Chandra said calmly. "I came here because you said that if I proved myself, you'd recommend me for the COO position within five years. *That's* always been the brass ring for me. The reason I've put up with your brother's—"

"I know." Ethan held up a hand and sighed. "And I'm sorry I can't make that happen. But I can offer you a sizable salary increase to ease the blow."

"That won't be necessary," Chandra said coolly, enjoying the shock in Ethan's eyes.

"Are you saying you don't want the increase?" he said. "Or are you saying—"

"I resign, effective immediately." Chandra stood tall and tipped her chin, meeting Ethan's gaze.

Ethan's shoulders sank. He dragged a hand down his face, which suddenly looked more haggard. "You don't need to do this, Chandra. My nephew probably won't last in this job for an entire year. That'll buy me some time to show my family how valuable you are to this organization and why you're so deserving of the COO position."

"It won't change the fact that I'm not a Phillips. And if your family hasn't realized my value by now, Ethan, I doubt they ever will." Chandra lifted her purse and laptop bag onto her shoulder. "Now, should I call security to meet me at my desk? I just need to grab my family photos and a few plants."

"No, I trust you, Chandra," Ethan said wearily, shoving his hands in his pockets. "Go. Do whatever you need to do."

Chandra took a few steps toward the door, then turned back to the man who was now her former boss. "Thank you for all you've done, Ethan. Have a safe return to Nashville."

"I'll show you where your things were moved." Evelyn gave Chandra a subtle nod and smile, as if cheering on her decision.

Evelyn accompanied Chandra to the smaller, dimmer office where her things had been set up. Then the other woman wished her the best of luck and took her leave.

Chandra used one of the moving boxes left behind to box up her family photos, a few plants and the small personal items stored in her desk. She reset her phone to factory and left it and her work-issued laptop on the desk.

She held her head high as she strolled to the elevator and got on, watching the doors close on Phillips Athletic Wear for the last time.

On the lobby level, she barely made it into a bathroom stall before she threw up everything she'd eaten that morning. She washed her hands and popped a piece of gum in her mouth, hoping it would ease her nervous stomach. Then she made her way to the parking garage.

The words *I resign* had escaped her mouth before she had time to reconsider them. But Chandra knew she'd made the right decision.

If she was going to devote all her time and energy to minding the interests of someone's family, it would be her own. So if her father was willing to agree to her terms, she'd be back in Magnolia Lake with her dad and brother and sister and the good doctor whom she couldn't seem to get out of her head.

When Julian had asked her to stay, she'd desperately wanted to say yes. But she'd permitted her relationship fears, her hang-ups about the difference in their ages and her misguided need to prove her worth outside of her family to hold her back. It was a mistake she wouldn't make again.

Fifteen

Three Weeks Later

Julian stepped out of his office and zipped his jacket against the chilly December air blowing down Main Street.

The new light posts, designed to look like antiques, were festively decorated with pine wreaths bound with red velvet bows. White fairy lights wound down each pole. Each shop on Main Street was decorated for the holidays. A towering Douglas fir was decked out over at the town square. By the time he left his office for the day, all the lights were twinkling, casting their ethereal glow over the town.

Julian had to admit that he'd enjoyed accompanying his mother to the official town lighting of the Christmas tree for the first time since his father's death. His father had loved Christmas, and the town's tree lighting had always been his dad's favorite event of the year. It hadn't seemed right to attend the event without him, so neither Julian nor his mother had.

He'd been stunned when his mother suggested they attend the event together. Julian had wanted to decline, but going to the tree lighting seemed really important to his mom. As it turned out, it was important for him, too.

Julian and his mother had stood on the festively decorated public square, surrounded by the people who comprised the town his father had adored. Attending the event that had always brought his father so much joy had been surprisingly cathartic.

She'd slipped her arm through his and it felt like they were finally grieving for his dad *together*. An essential part of the process if there was ever any hope of healing the rift between them. Neither one of them had talked about the past or the awkward nature of their current relationship. But they were both making an effort.

It wasn't always pretty, and sometimes it felt like he was pulling shards of glass from his skin. But things were slowly getting better between Julian and his mother.

His dad would've liked that. He would've liked Chandra, too.

Julian shoved a hand in his pocket and strolled across the street to the café that still held memories of Chandra.

He couldn't help thinking of Chandra's stunning smile. And the laugh that made him feel like he was floating in the balmy Caribbean Sea, his face warmed by the sun. The deep sense of happiness he felt whenever he was with Chandra. Despite the challenging logistics, Julian was convinced something genuine was happening between them.

He'd been hopeful when he'd asked if he could call her in San Diego, and she'd agreed. They'd chatted on the phone and exchanged text messages with increasing frequency during the first month after she left town. But three weeks ago, she'd sent him a cryptic message about something having come up and her being busy. Then suddenly, her line was no longer in service, and he felt like a complete ass.

Had she felt the need to change her number to get rid of him? Had she found someone else?

All Chandra had needed to do was say the word, and he would've respected her wishes. He hated to think that she'd felt it necessary to take such a drastic step to cut ties between them. And he couldn't bear her thinking poorly of him when he adored her and still wanted her in his life.

Julian pushed open the door to the café and greeted a few locals, including Mr. and Mrs. Donaldson—who was doing much better on her new blood pressure meds. Then he got in line.

"Hi, Julian."

Stunned, he turned his attention to the two women at the register. "Chandra? Naya?"

"It's really good to see you, Julian." Chandra tucked her hair behind her ear and smiled. She waved him forward. "I already added your pastrami sandwich to our order."

He joined Chandra and Naya at the head of the line, but when he tried to pay, she waved him off.

"My treat," Chandra insisted. "I was hoping we could talk."

"Of course." It felt surreal that she was there asking him to chat moments after he'd been wondering if he'd ever see her again.

"Actually, there's somewhere I need to be. Could you make my salad to go with the dressing on the side and have it ready in about an hour?" Naya asked the cashier before turning back to the two of them. "By then, you two should be done with lunch, right?" A mischievous smile lit Naya's face.

They both nodded in agreement.

Naya slid her expensive shades off her head and put them on. She ran her fingers through her purple bob and strutted out the door.

Julian and Chandra stepped aside to wait for their order. An awkward silence settled between them.

"So how have you been?" they asked at once. They both laughed, and it seemed to alleviate some of the awkwardness.

"You first." He gestured.

"Things have been...good." Chandra shifted her gaze around the space, then back to him. "How about you?"

"You know, still settling in." His gaze locked with hers. "Mostly missing you."

A shy smile curved her full lips. "Same."

"I'm really surprised to hear that." Julian rubbed his chin. "I mentioned that I'd like to fly out to San Diego to visit you after the New Year. Then suddenly you change your phone number. I assumed—"

"I didn't change my number because of you, Julian."

Chandra placed a hand on his arm. "And I'm sorry you thought I was ghosting you. I wasn't."

"Then why did you change your number?" He studied the lovely face that he'd practically memorized in the three weeks she'd been in town.

"That wasn't my personal phone… It was a company phone. I returned it when I resigned from my position."

"You quit your job in San Diego? When? Why? How long have you been in town? And how long are you staying?" He rattled off the questions as quickly as they came to his mind.

"I quit three weeks ago because I realized they didn't deserve me and never would," she said. "It took me a couple of weeks to pack up my things and put my house up for sale. I've been here about a week, and I'll be here indefinitely because I've accepted my father's offer to be the CEO of Valentine Vineyards."

"That's amazing. Congrats." Julian hugged her. "Still doesn't explain why you didn't call."

"Me resigning…it all happened so suddenly. I didn't think to write down your number or anyone else's before I handed in my phone." Chandra lowered her gaze to her clasped hands. "Thankfully, after the accident, I saw the need to at least memorize my father's and sister's numbers."

"That explains why you didn't have my number," Julian acknowledged. "But there's this thing…it's called the internet. You could've looked up my office number. Or you could've come by the office or the cabin since you've been back. Why didn't you?"

"Well, this is the third time this week I've come here for lunch at one," she admitted with a shrug. "I didn't want to ambush you at your office or just show up at the cabin. And to be honest…" Chandra glanced around the café. Her gaze landed on the table where Deanna Jasper and a few of her friends sat watching them. "We agreed to a fling when I was in town for a couple weeks. Now that I'm here permanently…I didn't want you to feel pressured into making this something…more. After all, you are Magnolia Lake's hottest bachelor. Every unattached woman in town seems to be pursuing you." Chandra tipped her chin in Deanna's direction.

"I haven't thought about anyone but you since the moment I met you." Julian looped an arm around Chandra's waist and tipped her chin. His mouth met hers in a slow, lingering kiss.

"Same," she said again, when he forced himself to end the kiss. He could practically feel the heat radiating from her cheeks as Mr. and Mrs. Donaldson and a few of the other patrons grinned at them.

"There's something else bothering you, isn't there?" Julian threaded their fingers as he searched her face.

"I know I shouldn't care what other people think. But I also don't want everyone in town staring at me like they are now…thinking of me as some cougar who set her sights on the town's beloved prodigal son."

"I hate the term *cougar*. That's some sexist bullshit. Older men have been dating younger women since the beginning of time. And as for them…" He nodded toward the Donaldsons but lowered his voice. "They're staring because they're well-meaning but also nosy as hell. This is the equivalent of a Shonda Rhimes primetime drama for most of them. But as much as they enjoy juicy drama, they're good people. And they're rooting for us, just like they're rooting for your family to make a success of Valentine Vineyards."

Julian breathed a small sigh of relief when Chandra smiled.

"When I'm with you, Chandra, the last thing in the world I'm thinking about is the difference in our ages. I'm thinking about how beautiful you are. How intelligent you are. How much I laugh when we're together. How my heart races whenever I see you. How much you've sacrificed for your family."

Julian cradled her face, grazing her cheek with his thumb. "And I'm envious of every person you've ever cared about."

Chandra's brown eyes shone. A smile crinkled the corners of her mouth. "You're very persuasive, Dr. Brandon. Anyone ever tell you that?"

Julian kissed her forehead. "And irresistible."

"And so very modest." Chandra giggled.

"True." Julian tightened his grip on her hand. "I don't care what anyone thinks about what we have. All I care about is being with you."

"Well, I *do* care about a few other things." A slow grin spread across her lips. "World peace. Global warming. Racial equality. This 'empire' my family is apparently building…"

"All right, point taken." Julian shook his head. "But I'm assuming I make the list."

"Oh, you definitely make the list." Chandra lifted onto her toes and kissed him.

Everyone behind the counter and several of the customers who'd been watching hooted and clapped.

"All right, you two lovebirds." Amina Lassiter, the

owner of the café, grinned as she shoved a tray toward them. "Your order is ready."

Julian thanked the woman and grabbed their order. They slid into a booth near the back of the café.

"So what prompted you to accept your dad's offer?"

Chandra set her sandwich down after taking one bite, as if she'd suddenly lost her appetite.

"It became abundantly clear that no length of service or list of accomplishments would ever earn me a spot on the Phillips Athletic Wear executive team." Chandra sipped her soda thoughtfully before setting down the cup. "It was foolish of me to be obsessed with proving my worth outside of my family, only to end up working myself ragged to cement the legacy of someone else's family. If I'm shedding blood, sweat and tears, I want it to be for the people who matter most to *me*." She slapped a hand to her chest. "The people I know I can always count on, no matter what—my family."

"Good for you." Julian smiled. "Besides, you really seemed to enjoy helping your dad and sister with setting things up at the winery."

"I did." Her face lit up.

Julian's heart skipped a beat. It still didn't feel real that Chandra was there with him.

"Let's hope I'm still excited about all of this once I officially begin in my role as CEO at the beginning of the year." Chandra took another tentative nibble on her sandwich.

"Did you enjoy working with your family at the textile firm?" Julian asked between bites of his sandwich.

"I enjoyed working with my father and brothers. My grandmother? Not so much." Chandra frowned. "She was brilliant and focused, but very old-school. I think she believed that if we enjoyed our work, we must be doing it wrong."

Chandra set her sandwich down after a few bites and pressed a hand to her forehead.

"Are you all right?" he asked.

"I've been feeling a little run-down lately. Undoubtedly the stress of uprooting my life and taking a chance on my dad's dream. Plus, it's my dad's birthday this weekend. So all of my brothers are coming into town."

"You've been feeling run-down *how*?" Julian asked, the wheels turning in his head.

"Headaches, nausea, fatigue, insomnia, moodiness." She shrugged.

"Sweetheart, you don't think you could be...?"

Chandra's eyes widened with recognition. She mouthed the word *pregnant* and he nodded.

"That's impossible!" she said in a loud whisper. "We were careful. You wore a condom every single time."

"True. But they aren't infallible," he noted. "Few things in life are."

"No. No way. I had my *period*—" she mouthed the word "—soon after I returned to San Diego. It wasn't as heavy as usual. But I did have it."

"And since?" Julian tried not to sound like a doctor questioning his patient.

"I haven't..." Chandra paused. "But I'm thirty-nine. They've been irregular the past few months. I assumed I was entering—"

"Perimenopause," he offered.

Chandra covered her face and groaned. "Not a conversation you want to have with your much younger lover."

"Boyfriend," he corrected. This was about far more than sex for either of them. "Who happens to be a doctor and is also mature enough to realize that it's a natural part of life." He squeezed her hand again, and she seemed relieved. "Your theory is possible, of course. But given the other symptoms you've described..."

"I'm not *that*." Chandra glanced around anxiously. "I haven't been with anyone else, and I just told you, I've had a period since we were together."

"Bleeding isn't as uncommon as you might think, especially in the first tri—"

"Stop talking like I'm..." Chandra couldn't seem to bring herself to say the word. "I think I'd know if I was."

"You'd be surprised how many women don't know they are." On the outside, Julian was calm and objective with his questions, as he was when speaking with a patient in the exam room. But inside, his heart beat wildly in his chest and his stomach did flips as he considered the very real possibility that he and Chandra had created more than just sparks during those steamy nights at his cabin.

"Well, I'm not," Chandra said with finality. She picked up her sandwich and bit into it. Suddenly, she looked like she was going to lose her lunch at any moment, much as she had the day they'd first met on the plane. But she continued to chew slowly, as if to prove a point.

Maybe Chandra was right. She would know her own body better than he, despite the fact that he'd committed every delicious curve and dimple to memory.

He was just glad she'd returned to Magnolia Lake

and that she was willing to give them a chance. He wouldn't blow it by pressing the issue.

"I want to hear how things are going with you and your mom." She set down the sandwich.

"We've been spending more time together. Last weekend we actually went to the town Christmas tree lighting ceremony together. The event was a huge deal for my dad. He'd transform into this oversize kid once they hit the lights on the town square." A sad smile curved Julian's mouth. "It was the first time Mom or I have attended the tree lighting since Dad died."

"Julian, that's amazing." Chandra grasped both his hands. "I'm really happy to hear that."

"Thanks." He kissed the back of her hand, his gaze locked with hers. "And I'm *really* glad you're here."

"Me, too." Her eyes danced and her skin practically glowed. "Now tell me how things are going with the new practice."

They talked about how the past few weeks had gone, and how he'd begun to win over a few of the diehards. Then Chandra told him what'd happened with the Phillips brothers back in San Diego and updated him on what was going on at the winery, her eyes sparkling with excitement as she shared the new branding and some of their plans.

"You have patients waiting back at the office." Chandra checked her watch, then shielded a yawn. "Go. We'll finish talking later."

"You're exhausted, aren't you?" Julian noted.

"I'm accustomed to living alone," Chandra said. "Now I'm staying with my dad, Nolan and Naya at the winery. Between my dad and brother, who are early risers, my sister—who talks incessantly and whose voice carries—all of the noises inherent in the wine-making process and the construction crew working on the house…getting any sleep in during the day is impossible. And I'm not getting the best sleep at night either." She yawned again. "My brothers are flying in for Dad's party and Nyles will probably stay through Christmas. So I doubt I'll get much sleep the next few nights either."

"Go to my cabin. You'll have the place to yourself for the next four hours. I'll text you a code to the door."

Chandra's eyebrows knitted together as she contemplated his offer. Finally, she nodded. "Thank you, Julian."

The woman he'd fallen head over heels for would be sleeping in his bed while he continued seeing patients. *Not distracting at all.*

Chandra exhaled quietly and gripped his hand. "Julian, I haven't done this in a while, and if I'm being honest, I'm still a little gun-shy."

"It's okay." He squeezed Chandra's hand. "Like I said, we'll take this as fast or as slow as you'd like. I'm not going anywhere. All right?"

Chandra nodded. "Thanks for understanding."

Julian gave her a quick kiss goodbye. Then he made his way across the street, wondering how he'd gotten so damn lucky.

Sixteen

Chandra paced the great room floor at Julian's cabin. Her heart thudded in her chest, her pulse raced and she felt light-headed.

When the front door swung open, Chandra nearly jumped out of her skin.

She should've heard Julian's SUV pull up or the turn of the front door lock. But apparently, she hadn't been able to hear anything over the thrum of the rushing blood that echoed in her ears.

"I'm sorry, sweetheart. I didn't mean to startle you." Julian set a bag on the counter.

The smell of the meal from the King's Finest Family Restaurant should have made her mouth water. Instead, she felt queasy. And now she knew why.

"Hey, you sure you're okay?" Julian placed the back of his hand to her forehead. Then he tipped her chin and studied her face. "I was hoping you'd get some rest. But you seem—"

"Pregnant." She cut him off. "Very, *very* pregnant. I don't know how you could've known when I didn't, but you were right. I had Naya stop at the drugstore before she dropped me here. I've taken two different pregnancy tests. They're both positive." Chandra could still hardly believe how her life, already in transition, had been turned upside down in a few hours.

"How are you—"

"I know this isn't what either of us expected from this relationship... But I do want this baby." Chandra placed a protective hand over her belly. "I realize fatherhood wasn't on the agenda, so I'll understand if you want to walk away. Keeping and raising the baby is my decision, and I'm prepared to deal with the consequences."

Julian blinked and seemed to come out of his momentary daze. He pulled her into his arms and kissed the top of her head. "I was going to ask how you're feeling."

"Oh." She'd been sure he was asking how she'd planned to deal with the pregnancy. "I'm fine. Just stunned. We were both so careful. I honestly didn't see this coming, and I swear I had no idea before I took that test this afternoon."

"Chandra, I believe you." Julian cupped her cheek, his reassuring gaze meeting hers. "And it's okay to be a little frightened and overwhelmed by this."

"Why would I be overwhelmed? I've managed business professionals most of my career, and I practically raised my brothers and sister. I'm more than capable of caring for this child."

Chandra didn't care that she sounded defensive. It was better than the alternative: being vulnerable and in a position to be hurt. Something she promised herself she'd never do again.

After all this time, the sting of Edward's rejection and the humiliation of his betrayal were still lodged beneath her skin, like the insidious cockleburs that stuck to her clothing and pricked her tender flesh when she and her brothers played in the field as kids.

"I've delivered my fair share of babies during my residency. Doesn't mean I'm not terrified at the thought of having a kid of my own. But we'll get through this. Together. Because I'll be there every step of the way."

Her heart swelled at Julian's heartfelt promise. Because despite her bravado, Chandra was definitely panicking. Julian recognized the vulnerability and fear in her eyes, and he'd stepped in to reassure her. Just as he'd done aboard the plane.

Julian was a genuinely good guy. Had he promised to be there for her and the baby strictly out of a sense of duty? If so, he'd undoubtedly come to resent that obligation. Eventually, he'd resent her and maybe even their child. And that was a thought she couldn't bear.

Chandra pulled free of Julian's embrace. A chill surrounded her immediately, despite the warm blaze of the fireplace.

"You're here because you have to be, Julian. We both know you're counting the days until you can return to Philadelphia. The last thing you want is a kid tying you to this place." Chandra slipped her hand in his. "Don't do this because you feel you have to, Julian. I can take care of this baby myself."

"I don't doubt it." Julian wrapped her in a hug and kissed her forehead. "Maybe parenthood wasn't part of either of our immediate plans, but I'm just as invested in this child as you are. So I'm not going anywhere, Chandra. If you're in, I'm in. Got it?"

Chandra nodded, tears gliding down her cheeks. She wiped at them, embarrassed. Less than twenty-four hours into parenthood and she'd already been reduced to tears.

"Everything will be fine, sweetheart. I promise."

When Julian's firm lips met hers in a kiss, Chandra melted into him. She gripped the lapels of his jacket.

What had begun as a source of comfort quickly blossomed into a heated embrace that set her skin on fire and made her belly flutter.

Julian shrugged his coat onto the floor, and she tugged the hem of his shirt from his waist and fumbled with the buttons as they continued their heated kiss. She dropped his shirt to the floor, followed by her own. Julian unzipped her skirt and it pooled at her feet. He gripped her bottom tight, his hardened length pinned between them, then lifted her. Chandra wrapped her legs around his waist as he transported her to his bedroom. The place where, perhaps, they'd conceived this child.

The thought sent a chill up her spine, her body tingling with desire for this man who'd come to mean so much to her.

She would never have imagined they'd end up here: about to be parents. But as Julian set her on her feet, and they fumbled to finish undressing one another amid their increasingly urgent kisses, she couldn't regret a single moment that had led them here.

They climbed into his bed, Julian's hands roaming

her bare skin. Their kisses escalating as the heat built between them until she felt as if she would combust.

When Julian reached for the drawer beside his bed, Chandra grabbed his wrist. "If you really haven't been with anyone since we were together…"

"I haven't," he assured her.

"Then I don't think we'll be needing what's in that drawer for a while." She caressed his stubbled cheek and pressed a soft kiss to his lips.

Julian's eyes darkened, his mouth curving in a wicked grin. "No, I suppose we won't."

He made love to her. Worshipped the body that would soon swell and sag and be marked with even more stretch marks as it nurtured the baby they'd made.

Chandra had no idea what the future would bring. Maybe Julian would never look at her again with the passion and hunger she saw in his eyes now. But she would enjoy these moments and commit them to memory. His taste. The weight of his body on hers. The sensation of him filling her. And the tender moments as he held her afterward and assured her everything would be all right.

Seventeen

Julian held Chandra, her cheek pressed to his chest and her dark hair draped across his arm, as she slept. Being with Chandra was always incredible. But tonight, their impassioned connection—with no barrier between them, knowing they'd created life together—had been unlike anything he'd experienced. Intoxicating. Addictive. Soulbinding. Every kiss, every touch felt so much more consequential.

After they'd spent the evening getting reacquainted with each other's bodies and bringing each other intense pleasure, he'd reheated their abandoned meals from the King's Finest Family Restaurant. A Blake's Steak and a loaded baked potato for him. A Cole Slaw Burger and seasoned fries for her. They'd eaten in bed while watching TV, and soon afterward, Chandra had fallen asleep. She seemed absolutely exhausted.

Julian had let her sleep while he showered, unloaded the dishwasher and did laundry. Then he'd climbed back into bed, cradling her to him as he obsessed over his new reality.

I'm going to be a father.

All of his unspoken fears raced through his brain. Would Chandra be okay? Would the baby? How would this arrangement work? Was he prepared to be a father—a really good one, like his own?

But the longer he lay there, thoughts of the future churning in his head, he was crystal clear about the future he envisioned for himself and the little family they'd suddenly become.

"Julian, are you okay?" Chandra lifted her head and wiped the sleep from her beautiful brown eyes. "Your heart is racing."

"I'm fine," he said, despite his heart hammering in his chest. "I've just been thinking."

"About?" Chandra folded her arms on his chest, her chin propped on the back of her hand as she stared up at him looking more enticing than ever.

All of the eloquent words Julian had planned to say lodged in his parched throat, and his mind went blank.

Chandra's expression fell and her brows furrowed. But she mustered a smile and stroked his cheek. "It's okay, Julian. I know you feel the need to do right by this baby. But becoming a parent is my choice, not yours. So if you'd rather not be involved—"

"Marry me, Chandra." Julian blurted the words out as the sound of the blood rushing filled his ears.

"Did you just ask me to *marry* you?" Chandra sat

up against the headboard, dragging the sheet up over her bare breasts.

Maybe he hadn't done this before, but he was pretty damn sure that wasn't the face of a woman who welcomed his marriage proposal. "Yes."

"Julian, you barely know me." She climbed out of the bed and slipped on her lacy black panties, then picked up the rest of her clothing and put it on—starting with her bra. "I'm some random chick you sat next to on the plane. The only reason we're here right now is because we're both apparently incompetent when it comes to birth control."

Julian climbed out of bed and slid his arms around Chandra's waist. He pulled her to him, halting her frantic attempts to get dressed.

"I need to be clear about something," he said. "No, I wasn't looking for a relationship when we met. But I agreed to a fling because that's all you were interested in. If you'd said you were only interested in a serious relationship that could lead to marriage and kids…I wouldn't have said no to that either." He dropped a kiss on her shoulder. "I was already too far gone."

Chandra's expression softened, but she still seemed anxious. "You're an amazing man, Julian. And I care very much for you. But marriage is the very opposite of taking this thing slowly."

"I know, but with the baby coming…it feels like we've vaulted past the taking-it-slow stage, right?" He gave her a small smile, and the tension in her back eased.

"Marriage is a serious commitment, Julian." Chandra seemed to be fighting a smile.

"It is," he agreed. "And even in the best of circum-

stances, marriage has a fifty-fifty shot of being successful. But I want to be a part of this child's life and yours.
I wanna be the kind of dad who will *always* be there.
The kind of dad I had and that you have. I'm ready to
prove that. Right here. Right now."

"I'd never keep you from being a part of our child's
life." She stroked his cheek. "But getting married just
for the sake of the baby… That isn't necessary, Julian.
My dad has *two* broken marriages that prove kids alone
won't equate to an enduring union."

"I realize that."

The pain in Chandra's eyes broke Julian's heart. He
wasn't sure who'd had it worst: him because his father
had been taken from him tragically, or her because her
mother and stepmother had willingly walked away.

"We've both suffered irrevocably in the absence of a
parent. I don't want that for our kid, Chandra. Do you?"

"Of course not. But I don't think we should get married just because I'm pregnant either." She placed a
hand on her belly.

"Obviously, the timing is prompted by news of the
baby. But I wouldn't ask you to marry me if I didn't
genuinely *want* to be with you, Chandra."

"Julian, you don't need to pretend that—"

"That I haven't been able to get you out of my head
since the day we met? That I've been in heaven with
you these past few months? And you're the only woman
I've ever considered a future with? Because every single
word of that is true."

Chandra stared at him, blinking. "But we just met a
few months ago." Her protest was weakening, her objection unsure.

"I know." Julian squeezed her hand, his eyes locked with hers. "But the moment you slipped your hand into mine on that plane…I swear I was a goner. It felt like I'd been waiting my entire life to meet you."

Chandra's eyes were suddenly glossy with unshed tears. She laughed nervously. "You really are persuasive, Dr. Brandon."

"Don't forget irresistible."

"And still modest." She shot a playful punch to his arm.

Julian chuckled. "Does that mean you're saying yes to my earnest, if slightly unconventional marriage proposal?"

"It means I'll give it serious consideration." Her sweet smile made his chest swell. "And that I feel the same about you."

Julian's smile widened. Maybe it wasn't a yes, but it wasn't no, and Chandra had admitted to having feelings for him. It gave him hope. "That's all I ask."

"Now, I have a question for you," Chandra said.

"Shoot."

"Whatever our relationship turns out to be," she said tentatively, "this will be our first Christmas together. I'd like to get you something really special. So maybe give me a little hint about what you want?"

A wide grin spread across Julian's face. "Chandra Valentine, all I want for Christmas is you."

"How very Mariah Carey of you." Her sexy smile ignited something in his chest. Chandra glided a hand down his side, awakening every single nerve ending in his body.

"What about you?" he asked.

Her deep brown eyes swam with emotion. She settled a hand on her belly. "You've already given me more than I could've ever hoped for. I honestly didn't think I'd ever… Thank you, Julian. For everything."

Julian captured her soft lips with his own, losing himself in her kiss and in the swell of emotions he felt whenever he was with this incredible woman. He pulled her back into his bed and made love to her again.

Regardless of Chandra's answer to his proposal, because of her, his life would never ever be the same again. And for that, he was grateful.

Eighteen

The following morning, Chandra stepped out of Julian's SUV, parked in the driveway of the Valentine Vineyards villa, as he held the door open for her. He leaned her against the back passenger door and gave her a dizzying kiss that evoked memories of the delicious, orgasm-inducing way he'd awakened her earlier that morning.

She clenched her thighs against the pulsing of her core.

"Meet me for lunch?" Julian nuzzled the side of her face with his scruffy cheek. His voice was gruff, much as it had been when he'd awakened that morning.

"I have a meeting with our winemaker, Maria, at one. But I'll make dinner at your place tonight. After all, you should know what you'd be getting yourself into." She grinned, then whimpered when he kissed the space behind her ear he knew drove her crazy. It sent a chill down her spine that had nothing to do with the frigid wind swirling down from the Smoky Mountains.

"Perfect. Just use the code to let yourself in." Julian kissed her temple. "This time, bring an overnight bag."

Chandra bit her lip and sighed. She hadn't intended to spend the night at Julian's. But she'd loved waking up to him, their limbs intertwined and him peppering her with kisses that began at her neck and ended with his head beneath the covers.

"I will." Her face and neck heated.

"Are you sure you don't want me to be there when you tell your family?" Julian's brows furrowed. "It only seems right that I be there."

My God, you're precious.

"I appreciate the offer." Chandra stroked his stubbled chin with her gloved hand. "But I'm a big girl. I can handle this. Besides, your first patient of the day is waiting."

"If you're sure." Julian tucked her arm into the crook of his elbow and walked her onto the back porch of the villa. He kissed her again, then jogged back to his running vehicle.

"God, that man is hot," Chandra whispered beneath her breath as she unlocked the back door and made her way inside.

"Well, look who decided to join us for breakfast after all." Her youngest brother stood from the breakfast table and gave her his signature bear hug.

Nolan, Sebastian and Alonzo were also at the table.

"I thought you all were coming in on Friday." Chandra tossed her coat on a nearby chair.

"We wanted to surprise you by coming in a couple

days early." Sebastian's thick eyebrows lifted, his judgment face firmly in place.

No time like the present.

"Speaking of surprises…" Chandra glanced around the table. "I'm glad you're here early. There's something I need to tell you."

"All right." Her father's wiry gray brows knitted with concern. "Have a seat and tell us what's on your mind."

"Actually, I'd rather stand." Chandra tightened her grip on the back of the empty chair, suddenly needing its support. "It seems that I…uh…am…pregnant." She spread her hands, as if she'd just said…*Ta-da!*

They all stared in silence, as if awaiting the punch line of an ineptly told joke.

"Wait…you're serious?" Alonzo asked, finally. "Sis, you're like *the* most responsible person I have ever known. No offense, Pops."

"None taken," her father said. Though, by the furrow of his brow, there clearly was.

Alonzo didn't seem to notice. "How on earth did you—"

"We're good, Zo." Nolan held up a hand. "I'm pretty sure Dad gave everyone here the *where do babies come from* speech."

"Not me. If it was up to Dad, I'd still think we were all delivered by the stork." Naya narrowed her gaze at their father. "But I would like to take this time to say… *Yay!* I'm going to be an auntie. Also, you all were so sure *I* would be the one who'd get knocked up," Naya added gleefully. "Ha!"

"Not now, baby girl," her father warned.

"Fine," Naya muttered as their father and brothers glared.

Alonzo dragged a hand over his head, looking as stunned as he'd been when he'd discovered that their father was the real tooth fairy. "And you've obviously decided—"

"Yes," Chandra said firmly. She cupped a hand over her belly protectively. "This might be my only chance to have a child. I'm nearly forty, and I'm not involved with anyone—"

"With respect, sis, *clearly* you have been." Sebastian pointed his fork in her direction.

Her cheeks burned.

Chandra was a womanist and she certainly wasn't a prude. Still, she couldn't help feeling a little embarrassed to have this conversation with her father and brothers. Talking about her sex life and the child now growing inside her...this was new territory for all of them. "Point taken, Bas."

"I didn't realize you wanted kids." Nolan's tone and expression softened. "You've never really talked about having children."

"I guess I didn't realize how much I wanted to be a mother until I discovered I was pregnant."

The range of emotions Chandra had gone through when one pregnancy test, then the other had turned positive replayed in her head. She'd gone from abject fear, to confusion, to the slow realization that she wanted to be a mother. A desire she'd carefully suppressed after her failed engagement.

"I've been so focused on my career the past few

years. And prior to my engagement, I wasn't even sure I... I mean—"

"You didn't know if you wanted kids after having to practically raise all five of us." There was a hint of apology or maybe guilt in Alonzo's voice.

Chandra's gaze swept the room. Alonzo's sentiments were echoed in the expressions on Nolan's, Sebastian's, Nyles's and Naya's faces. As if they felt guilty for somehow derailing her life. But nothing could be further from the truth. They'd taught her so much: love and patience; empathy and kindness. And they needed to know that.

"I'm glad I was able to be there for all of you. And I'm proud of who you've become. Nurturing each of you taught me so much. It made me who I am today," Chandra said with a warm smile. "Maybe I was reluctant to have kids of my own because it sometimes felt like I'd raised all of you. Not that Dad wasn't there," she added.

"That's sweet of you, Chandra." Her father rubbed a hand over his thinning hair. "But we all know I wasn't. Not the way I should've been. I guess that was another reason I was anxious to wash my hands of Valentine Textiles. My blind commitment to the company is part of the reason my marriages failed. And it's why I missed out on so much of your lives. I wanted to make my parents proud. But that's no excuse. You kids deserved better, and I'm sorry I didn't give it to you." There was a sheen over her father's eyes. "I don't know that I've ever really thanked you for the sacrifices you made for this family, sweetheart."

He squeezed her hand, a soft smile lighting his eyes. "So if this is what you want, every last one of us will

stand behind you and support you any way we can."
He shot Nolan, Sebastian and Alonzo a warning glare.
"Promise."

"Thanks, Dad." Warm tears slid down her cheeks.
She leaned down to hug her father.

"You know we've got you, sis. No matter what."
Alonzo offered her a crooked smile that reminded her
of when he was a kid and wanted to make amends.

Her siblings nodded their agreement, and she felt a
sense of relief.

"But what about the *good doctor*?" Sebastian said
the words with a hint of derision. "What does he think
of becoming a father?"

"I made it clear to him that this is my choice, and I
have no expectations for him to be a part of this child's
life or mine if that's not what he wants. Eighteen years
of child-rearing certainly wasn't the expectation of our
little fling," Chandra said carefully.

"Oh, you think raising kids is just an eighteen-year
gig, huh?" Her dad chuckled dryly. "That's cute."

Nolan laughed. "Yeah. How old are you two again?"
He gestured toward the twins. "Twenty-five?"

"Twenty-eight in a couple of months," Nyles corrected
him.

"And we resent that." Naya directed one of her long,
pointy colorful fingernails at Nolan. "I'm an adult, and
I take care of myself just fine, thank you."

"But you also ask Dad for shit…like all the time,"
Sebastian reminded her.

Naya's eyes narrowed. "Boy, mind yo' business—"

"Nolan and Sebastian, would you two please leave
your sister alone?" Her father glared at them. "Besides,

I like doing things for you kids. Makes me feel like you still need me. Can't blame an old man for wanting to feel needed."

"Dad, I will *always* need you. Clearly." Chandra pressed a hand to her belly. "More than ever once the baby is born."

Her father practically beamed. "You know I'll be there with anything you need."

"But will the baby's father be there? Or did he take the option to dip, which you so conveniently offered?" Sebastian Valentine was like a beagle with a bone. He never got off track and wasn't easily distracted, which had made him the perfect operations manager at Valentine Textiles. The trait was far less appealing in a sibling.

Chandra didn't owe any of them an explanation. And she didn't need to justify what she'd done or her plans for the future. But she couldn't bear her family thinking poorly of Julian when he'd been nothing but supportive.

"He's in, one hundred percent. He even…" Chandra drew in a shaky breath, not sure she should tell them everything. But the words rushed from her lips. "Julian asked me to marry him."

"You're kidding me!" Naya rushed over to Chandra. "You must've been completely shocked."

"I was. I still am stunned by all of this." Chandra felt like she was in a wildly vivid dream.

Her father rubbed his chin and nodded, seemingly pleased by Julian's act of chivalry.

"You hardly know each other," Alonzo noted. "Don't get me wrong—you're an amazing catch, and he'd be damn lucky to have you. But I'm surprised he'd go straight for marriage."

"Me, too," she admitted. "I assured him I'd never come between him and our child, if he wants to be part of their life. But he doesn't want to be a part-time dad. And this isn't just about the baby for him." Chandra's cheeks warmed. "He seems genuinely excited about the prospect of us being together."

"Could Julian have a possible motive—besides the baby and wanting to be with you?" Sebastian pressed.

Chandra paced the floor, more than a little irritated.

Did her brother actually believe a man would have to have some ulterior motive in order to propose to her?

She was trying to be patient with her brothers. They only wanted to protect her; she realized that.

"I don't believe he has a motive other than wanting to be a fully present, full-time father to our child. We all know how devastating it is to have a parent walk away. Julian's experience wasn't the same as ours, but he lost a parent, too. He knows how much it hurts."

She'd never forget the trauma of her mother abandoning them. It affected her even now. And she knew it still impacted each of her siblings. Especially her brooding brother Sebastian, who seemed determined to view the world as a glass half empty, and Nyles, who pretended nothing really mattered.

"Not me." Nyles's vehement protest was punctuated by a bitter laugh. "We're better off without our mother. Didn't need her then, don't need her now."

A collective sadness seemed to wash over the room, but no one countered her youngest brother's claim.

"The general consensus around town seems to be that the young doc is a good, honorable man." Her father redirected the conversation. "And let's not forget that he genuinely seems to care for your sister."

"True." Nolan nodded thoughtfully. He sipped his mimosa. "He asks about you every time I see him in town."

"Same." Her father chuckled.

"Of course he does. Because he *clearly* has a thing for her." Naya wagged a finger at Alonzo and Sebastian. "I swear the man looks like he's about to die with happiness every time he looks in your eyes." Naya grinned. "It's fucking adorable."

"He said he was a goner the moment he met me on the plane. That it felt like he'd been waiting his entire life to meet me." A soft, dreamy smile turned up the corners of her mouth. Her cheeks burned and her chest tightened at the memory of the words spoken so sincerely. "I know it sounds corny to you and maybe you think it's foolish of me to believe him—"

"The young playa got game—I'll give him that," Sebastian muttered under his breath, and Nyles elbowed him.

"I don't think it's corny at all, and I believe him, too. Because that's exactly what I see in his eyes whenever he asks about you." Naya grinned, squeezing Chandra's hand. "The question is…did you accept his marriage proposal?"

"No. But I promised to give it serious consideration, and I will." Chandra rubbed the back of her neck. "Now, if you'll excuse me, I'm still a little tired. I'm going to take a nap. I'll see you all in a few hours."

Chandra left the room, her family silent until she

closed the door behind her. Then they all seemed to speak at once.

She was tempted to press her ear to the door and eavesdrop on their conversation about her shocking revelation. But what they all thought of her decision was their business—not hers.

She'd decided to have this baby—with or without Julian and with or without the support of her family. But her heart felt full, and a deep sense of relief washed over her at having both.

That was enough for now.

Nineteen

It wasn't quite five thirty in the evening, but the sun had already set when Julian pulled his SUV into his mother's driveway. He parked, then pulled out his phone, typing out a quick message to Chandra.

Made a quick stop at my mom's. Be home soon.

A flicker of joy bubbled in his chest at the thought of him and Chandra calling the same space *home*.

They hadn't discussed living together. That was his Plan B conversation if Chandra didn't accept his marriage proposal. Still, waking up with her in his arms that morning had been a slice of heaven. And knowing that the CEO-to-be mother of their child wanted to make him a meal and that she planned to spend another night in his bed made his usually cautious heart feel full in ways it hadn't before.

Julian had admittedly avoided making deep connections in his life, having learned early that the people he loved could be snatched away from him in a flash. And there was nothing he could do about it. But he'd felt an almost instant affinity for Chandra. And little by little, he'd been opening himself up to her and letting her in, and he was thankful that he had. Because being with her made him happier than he'd ever been.

When he knocked on the side door, his mother seemed pleasantly surprised to see him.

"I wasn't expecting you tonight." She opened the door to let him in. "I just made a gourmet grilled cheese sandwich for dinner, but I'd be happy to make you one."

"Thanks, Mom, but I'll only be a few minutes. Chandra is making dinner." He followed her into the kitchen, not missing the hitch in her step when he mentioned Chandra.

"So she's back in town." His mother pulled two bottles of water from the fridge and handed him one.

He opted to save his speech about the ecological dangers of bottled water and accepted it gratefully.

"Ray must be happy." She rubbed at her forehead and sighed quietly. A sure sign that she was carefully calculating how to phrase her next statement. "So I guess that means you two are back on?"

"We were never really off." Julian swigged water from the bottle. "It was more of a misunderstanding."

"Clear, frequent communication is vital in any relationship, son."

"Like ours?" Julian frowned, hiking an eyebrow.

His mother ignored the jab about their dysfunctional, though improving, relationship. She folded her arms and leaned against the edge of the counter. "I'm serious, Jules. It's difficult enough to keep the lines of communication open in a traditional relationship. But in a long-distance one—"

"Chandra accepted Ray's offer. She's going to be Valentine Vineyards' CEO." He tried, unsuccessfully, to strain the smugness from his tone. "She put her house in San Diego up for sale, and she's already moved here to Magnolia Lake. She's staying at the villa with her dad and sister."

"For now." It wasn't a question, so he didn't deny it.

"You just don't like Chandra." Julian set his water down. "You tolerated her because you thought she'd return to California and I'd move on."

"That isn't true." She set her bottle on the counter, then smoothed her hand over her shoulder-length salt-and-pepper gray hair, pinned up in a bun. "I like Chandra very much. She's sweet, thoughtful, accomplished. And my heart can't help but go out to a woman who's been through so much. Abandoned by her mother, stepmother and fiancé. Being tasked with practically raising her brothers and sister when she was only a kid herself."

"But—"

"But she is much older than you. Of course, there's no crime in that." She raised her palms to halt his objection. "But I think maybe you have different goals in life. You're a young man just beginning your career as a physician with an independent practice. Maybe you haven't given it much thought, but I'd imagine you'll eventually want to start a family. Chandra's nearly forty, right? So having kids might not be part of her trajectory, which is also fine. But that puts you two at—"

"Chandra's pregnant, Ma." Julian practically blurted out the words, punctuated by a nervous laugh.

He collapsed against the counter behind him after finally revealing the secret he'd carefully guarded all day. He hadn't intended to state it so bluntly without preamble. But he'd wanted to stop his mother's descent before she could dig herself any deeper with her *Chandra's too old to give me grandchildren* routine.

"I'm going to be a dad." Julian placed a palm over his heart, then dragged his fingers through his hair and shook his head. "I can still hardly believe it."

"So the news came as a shock, but isn't necessarily unwelcome." His mother nodded; her arms folded. "Is that why Chandra came back?"

"Neither of us knew before yesterday." Julian drank more of his water. "Chandra moved here to be a part of her family's new venture at the vineyards and to give this relationship a legitimate shot."

"Well, it's good you were at least part of the reason Chandra chose to relocate here." His mother propped her chin on one fist. "With a baby on the way, it'll be tempting to hurry your relationship along. But there's no reason you two can't still take your time and—"

"I asked Chandra to marry me." Julian rubbed the back of his neck and tried to ignore his mother's shocked expression.

"I see. And what did she say?"

"She's considering it. But regardless of her answer, I need you to understand that I care deeply for this woman. And I want her to be part of my life."

"Congratulations is in order, then, I suppose." She squeezed his arm and gave him a soft smile. "If this is what you both *truly* want, then I'm happy for you."

Now wasn't the time to unpack his mother's conditional congratulations. Then again…maybe it was.

"I came here tonight because I wanted you to be the first person I told about the baby and about asking Chandra to marry me. But I also came to say this… I want to be a good dad. No, a great one. Like Dad was. But I can't do that if I'm drowning in guilt and resentment over the way things have been between us since Dad died." A knot clenched in Julian's gut. "So we need to stop pretending like everything is fine and talk about this."

"I've been thinking about that a lot lately." His mother's brows furrowed, and her eyes were suddenly watery. She stared down at her clasped hands. "The state of our relationship…I realize it's my fault."

"I didn't come here to toss blame, Ma." He really hadn't. But he appreciated her acknowledging her role in all of this.

"You didn't toss blame, sweetheart. I'm just owning up to my mistakes. Something I should've done a long time ago." She sighed softly. "When you stopped coming home for the holidays, I said I didn't mind. But the truth was…I was devastated that my only child couldn't bear to endure Christmas with me. It forced me to reexamine my life and contemplate how royally I'd screwed up as a mother. I handled your father's death poorly. I was so consumed with my own grief and—"

"Blaming me for Dad's death?" Julian clutched the counter behind him, his forehead tensing.

"Yes," she whispered. The lines around her eyes seemed to age her a decade.

Julian had been ten and was running late for school and had missed the bus again. His mother insisted that he walk the two miles to school and endure detention for being late. But his dad had met him around the corner and given him a ride to school. Said it would be their little secret.

Julian had arrived at school just before the late bell rang, feeling smug because he'd outsmarted his mother. But the unplanned side trip made his father run late for work. His dad had been speeding when he hit an oil slick on the road and spun out, colliding with a logging truck. He'd been killed instantly.

Julian had revisited that day in his head again and again. Thought of all the things he would've done differently.

What if he'd heeded his mother's warning about staying up too late so he wouldn't oversleep? What if he'd laid his school clothes out the night before, as his mother had often admonished? What if he'd obeyed his mother and just walked to school that day?

Then his father would still be alive.

But he hadn't done any of those things. And though he hadn't caused his father's accident, had he been a more considerate, compliant son, his father would likely still be alive to celebrate the news of expecting his first grandchild.

"What happened to your father was an unfortunate accident." His mother's pained words broke into his thoughts. "I'm sorry for the irrational blame I laid at your feet. It was wrong of me. We were both grieving, and I should've been there for you instead of accusing you of…" She sucked in a deep breath, her lower lip wobbling. "I can't even imagine what a burden you must've been shouldering all this time. I'm so sorry, Jules."

"I appreciate that, Ma. But I didn't come here to revisit our painful history." He rubbed unconsciously at the ache in his chest. "I'm only interested in how we move forward from this."

"Maybe I can't make amends for the past. But if I don't at least try, we'll never break down this wall between us. And we'll never be able to build a bridge to a better future." His mother sniffled and swiped a knuckle beneath her glistening eyes. "When you didn't come home these past few years, it made me realize how much I've been missing out on your life. And I can't help thinking that if your father could see what's become of our relationship…it'd break his heart. This isn't what I want for us, sweetie."

"Me neither." Julian swallowed back the pain bubbling in his chest. "But after a while, I gave up." He shrugged. "It just seemed…hopeless."

She stepped forward and cupped his cheek, tears streaming down her face. "It isn't, I promise you. I didn't mention it before, but I started going to therapy a few months ago." She squeezed his hand. "I'm trying *really* hard to change. Please, be patient with me."

"I will." Julian pulled his mother into a hug. This was the most optimistic he'd been about their relationship in twenty years. "Love you, Ma."

"Love you too, son."

Julian's cell phone dinged with a text message. He read the message from Chandra.

We really need groceries.

True. But he loved that she'd said *we*.

When the three dots, indicating that she was writing a reply, danced on his phone, Julian's smile broadened.

Think your mom can spare cucumbers and tomatoes?

He showed his mother the screen.

"For the woman who's made my baby so happy and who's finally going to make me a grandmother? Anything." She winked, then rummaged in the fridge and handed him the requested vegetables. "My future daughter-in-law is waiting. You'd better get on home."

Julian kissed his mother's cheek and headed for the SUV, hoping she was right and that Chandra Valentine would agree to be his wife.

Twenty

Julian sang along to Mary J. Blige's "Family Affair" playing in the background as he stacked charcuterie trays in his refrigerator from the Magnolia Lake Bakery. He opened a case of imported beer and shoved the long-neck green glass bottles into a cooler on the floor. Then he unloaded the reusable grocery bags filled with chips, dip and other snacks onto the kitchen counter.

A few weeks ago, he'd mentioned to Cole Abbott how much he'd missed the monthly poker night he and his roommate had held back in Philly. Cole had grinned and asked if that was an invitation. Just like that, he'd been volunteered to host their first monthly poker night. He'd invited Cole and his brothers: Blake, Parker and Max; Cole's cousin Benji and brother-in-law Dallas; and Julian's cousins Elias and Ben from Gatlinburg.

Julian had been excited about hosting the game until Chandra returned to town a week and a half ago.

They'd been practically inseparable since then, and Chandra had spent every single one of those nights in his bed.

Julian had been captivated by Chandra before. But now he was obsessed with discovering everything there was to know about this incredible woman who'd taken his breath away and turned his world upside down. The woman who would be the mother of his child. A connection they would always share.

He understood the science behind pregnancy glow: fluctuating hormones, increased blood flow, elevated oil production, etc. But seeing Chandra practically lit from within—like the holiday lanterns in the town square—and more beautiful than ever was mesmerizing. He could barely keep his hands off her.

But as addicted as he'd become to her taste, her sweet honeysuckle scent, the scintillating heat of her soft brown skin, and the growing passion between them, he enjoyed the quiet moments they spent together even more. Cooking a simple meal. Watching television together. Sharing stories—both funny and poignant—about their childhoods. Peeling back the layers to reveal a little more of themselves to each other as she lay in his arms each night.

Being with Chandra had been everything he'd imagined and more. Julian looked forward to waking up to her every morning, and he was sure she felt the same. Still, she hadn't mentioned his marriage proposal, and he hadn't wanted to push her. Her words that day at the café echoed in his head.

Julian, I haven't done this in a while, and if I'm being honest, I'm still a little gun-shy.

He needed to convince Chandra he was nothing like her former fiancé. That he'd never abandon or betray her and the baby. That their life together could be truly amazing, if she'd give them a chance.

The crunch of gravel in the driveway drew his attention. Julian glanced at his watch. The guests weren't scheduled to arrive for another forty minutes. But maybe his cousins had come down earlier to catch up before the other players arrived.

Julian unlocked the front door, then did a final straightening of the space.

Multiple footsteps climbed the front steps. Then there was a banging on the front door.

"Come in!" Julian poured some pretzels in a bowl. "And why the hell are you knocking on my front door like…?" Julian halted midsentence when his eyes met the steely, narrowed gaze of Sebastian Valentine.

Sebastian stood, legs wide, with his arms folded. He wore his usual scowl. Alonzo stood beside him, looking just as displeased. Nolan and Nyles completed the ragtag posse.

"Nolan, Sebastian, Alonzo, Nyles." Julian widened his stance and folded his arms as he acknowledged the four men. "Wasn't expecting you guys. What's up?"

"It's about our sister," Nolan said.

"Is she all right?" Julian's heart thumped, prompted by the worried look on Nolan's face.

He and Chandra hadn't spoken since they'd had lunch at the café earlier that day. She'd been tired and slightly nauseous but nothing that raised a red flag.

"Yes, she's fine. But she's—"

"Knocked up. Maybe you've heard?" Sebastian's hands curled into fists at his sides.

"Right." Julian nodded.

At Chandra's insistence, he hadn't spoken to her family since they'd discovered she was pregnant. She wanted to give Sebastian and Alonzo, her two hothead brothers, a chance to cool down. Clearly, that strategy hadn't worked.

"If this is the part where you show up at my house with a shotgun and insist I make an 'honest woman' of your sister, maybe you missed the part where I already asked her to marry me."

"We know about the proposal." The calmness in Alonzo's voice belied the anger evident in his narrowed gaze and flared nostrils. "But we also know about all your shady little side hustles—the gambling, the real estate *investment* schemes, and let's not forget your history of dating wealthy older women." Alonzo held up another finger as he ticked off each "offense."

Whomever the Valentines had hired to look into him had done their homework. But they'd sold the fellas a lot more sizzle than steak.

Unlike his trust fund buddies, he couldn't just make a sizable withdrawal or ask Daddy for a loan when he wanted to go into real estate investment. So he'd made the seed money for his earliest joint ventures by playing Texas Hold'em and Seven-Card Stud.

In the beginning, he'd lost more than he'd won. But he'd studied both games. Watched the pros. Practiced every chance he got. It hadn't taken him long to turn things around, and he'd made a lot of money. Money he'd used to buy into investments that had made him a lot more money and were a lot less risky.

"You haven't told your sister about any of this," Julian said, keeping his expression neutral.

"I just bet you would prefer we keep this from Chandra." Sebastian practically snarled. "But if you think—"

"That wasn't a request, Sebastian." Julian stared the other man down. "It was a statement. You clearly haven't mentioned any of this to Chandra. Because if you had, she would've told you she already knew all of this. I genuinely care for your sister." He scanned the faces of all four brothers. "And I have no secrets from her. Nor am I ashamed of my humble beginnings or the hustle and grind I put in to make a comfortable life for myself." He shrugged. "Chandra and I talked about all of this *before* we learned about the baby. So I'm sorry if you wasted your dime on your little private investigator. But if you'd just asked, I would've told you anything you wanted to know."

"If part of that 'hustle and grind'—" Sebastian used air quotes "—is trying to marry our sister to get your hands on her share of the sale of Valentine Textiles, just know you won't see a dime. There's no way in hell I'm letting my sister marry a virtual stranger without an ironclad prenup."

"I'm pretty sure your sister does whatever the hell she wants," Julian said. "And I don't want or need Chandra's money. If your sister asks me to sign a prenup, as I would expect someone in her position to do, I'll sign it without hesitation. End of story." Julian shoved his hands in his pockets. "Anything else?"

"We realize that you're doing well financially, Dr.

Brandon." Nolan pushed his smudged glasses up the bridge of his nose. "I guess our concern is—"

"*How* you got that money," Alonzo interjected. "You have an affinity for wealthy older women."

"The kind that die and leave you a shitload of money," Sebastian added.

"So that's what this is about." Julian rubbed his jaw and sank onto a nearby bar stool.

As irritated as Julian was with the Valentine brothers for delving into his past, he admired how fiercely they were protecting their sister.

He tried to consider the situation from their perspective. Their sister meets a complete stranger on a plane—who happens to be a younger man. Within a few months of meeting her—and learning of her impending inheritance from the sale of their family's firm—she's pregnant and he's asking her to marry him. Then they discover he's inherited millions from an older woman before.

Maybe they were being a little melodramatic about it, but this was definitely beginning to sound like the setup to a murder mystery where he was the prime suspect.

"You want to know about my relationship with Meredith Valera and why she left me—"

"Four hundred million dollars," Sebastian and Alonzo said in stereo.

"Meredith Valera was determined to use her family's wealth to right wrongs and do some good in underserved communities. I volunteered at the rural and inner-city clinics her organization ran. We'd chat at the clinic and she'd sometimes consult me about different initiatives she planned to roll out."

Julian smiled at the memory of the kindhearted philanthropist who'd help him channel his pain and need for redemption into his volunteer work.

"When she became terminally ill, we talked about the legacy she wanted to leave and how her money-grubbing children and grandchildren would squander her wealth. But I was as shocked as anyone that she left that money to me along with strict instructions on how it should be distributed. I've honored her wishes and will continue to do so. I've never used a cent of that money for myself, nor will I."

Sebastian and Alonzo didn't look convinced.

"As for the other wealthy older woman you're referring to, we met through mutual friends and dated for a few months. It didn't work out. We both moved on. End of story. Sorry to disappoint you, but there was nothing nefarious about my relationship with either of them."

"So just to be clear, there are no murdered wives whose insurance you collected?" Nyles added.

"You guys really need to lay off the true crime shows." Julian shook his head and chuckled.

Nolan and Alonzo laughed, and Julian was pretty sure Sebastian smiled for about a microsecond before resuming his usual scowl.

"Hey, that shit happens." Nyles folded his arms. "I need to know what to look out for. I am not tryna end up with my face on an episode of *Snapped*."

Nolan shook his head. He shifted his gaze to Julian. "As you've probably determined, Chandra means a lot to us. She's been more than a sister. She's been like a mother to us."

"I know." Julian nodded. "She often talks about you all. I understand how much you all mean to her and why she must mean so much to you." Julian couldn't help smiling as he thought of Chandra's beautiful brown eyes and contagious laugh. Of the smile that made him feel like he was floating on air.

"Look, I'm by no means perfect. I've made a lot of mistakes in my life. Some of which I'm still trying to atone for. But I swear to you, I have no ulterior motives where your sister is concerned. Maybe I don't deserve her." Julian shrugged. "But I'm damn lucky she walked into my life, and I plan to spend the rest of it making her feel just as lucky she walked into mine."

The Valentine brothers stared at him, seemingly at a loss for words.

"Told you I liked this guy." Nyles nodded approvingly. "If you can't appreciate how beautiful that speech was, you're the Tin Man. You have no heart."

Sebastian elbowed his youngest brother in the ribs. "Whose side are you on, anyway?"

"Chandra's," Nyles, Alonzo and Nolan all answered simultaneously.

"C'mon, Bas. Chandra gave him every opportunity to walk away, and instead he asks her to *marry* him. Clearly, he's serious about her," Nolan said.

Sebastian frowned, still unconvinced. But the anger in his eyes dimmed, ceding to something softer: genuine love and concern for his sister.

"She's been through a lot. And she's sacrificed a lot. For all of us. Now she's doing it again. This time for my dad's dream of building a wine empire." Sebastian sighed. "She's caring and self-sacrificing. She hasn't always gotten the same in her relationships. We just don't want to see her get hurt again."

The tension in Julian's shoulders eased. Maybe Sebastian could be kind of an asshole. But the man obviously loved his sister and wanted to protect her. Julian respected that, even if he didn't agree with his approach.

"Chandra and I sort of bonded over the pain of losing a parent when we were young. And I know about the broken engagement. I understand what's at stake here, Sebastian. Chandra is this unexpected ray of light in my life. Being with her makes me happy. I just want to do the same for her. But no matter what she chooses to do, I will *always* be there for her and for the baby."

The front door burst open and the room was filled with the raucous laughter of Julian's cousins Elias and Ben.

"What's up, Jules? Everything good?" Elias sized up the four men standing in Julian's great room. His cousin's face had gone from jovial to fight-ready in two seconds flat.

"Yeah. We're good." Julian introduced Chandra's brothers to his cousins.

"Hello." Ben smiled brightly as he shook hands with each of them, oblivious to the tension in the room.

Elias tipped his chin warily. "Y'all here for poker night?"

"Poker night?" Nyles rubbed his hands together. His dark eyes sparkled. "Oh, so you just weren't going to invite us? That's wrong, bro. We're practically family."

"None of you were in town when we made plans for tonight." Julian didn't want to spoil poker night with the tension between him and Chandra's brothers. But now that they were there, he couldn't not invite them. "You're welcome to stay, of course."

Nolan inched toward the door. "Thanks, but we should probably—"

"We'd love to stay. It'll give us a chance to get acquainted," Alonzo said. "Like Nyles said, we're practically family."

"Mind if I open the pita chips?" Nyles held up the bag.

"Help yourself. I was about to empty the bag into a bowl."

A mischievous smile slid across Nyles's face. "Thanks... *Jules.*"

Julian narrowed his gaze at Chandra's youngest brother.

Just let it go.

He remembered how Chandra had described the oldest twin. *A jokester who is doing his best to cope with the deep trauma inflicted by his mother's abandonment.*

Julian wasn't sure how the rest of the night would go, but he wanted to marry Chandra. And whether she said yes or not, they'd agreed to raise this child together. Things would go much smoother if he could win over Chandra's brothers.

Tonight seemed like a good place to start.

Twenty-One

Chandra surveyed the driveway of Julian's cabin. Sebastian's car was there along with several others, including her cousin Cole's truck. Several other vehicles were parked along the road in front of the cabin.

Were her brothers clowning in front of half the town? Or had they enlisted their new cousins to intimidate Julian?

Either way, she was prepared to whip the entire lot of them. How dare they embarrass her like this?

"I need to find someplace to park," Naya said.

It was her sister who'd told her that while she was napping, her brothers had decided to go to the cabin and have a chat with Julian.

Chandra had tried calling him, but her calls had gone to voice mail. None of her brothers were answering their phones either. Chandra was so angry with Nolan, Sebastian, Alonzo and Nyles that her hands were shaking. So it was good her sister had insisted on driving her.

"Let me out here." Chandra released her seat belt and opened the door of her black Mercedes.

Naya grabbed her wrist. "Maybe take a deep breath before you go in."

"I will. Then I'll knock the four of their heads together if they've so much as breathed on Julian wrong."

"I think you're underestimating the man. He's more than capable of handling himself," Naya called to Chandra's back as she exited the car.

Chandra hurried up the drive and onto the porch. A crashing sound came from inside the cabin, followed by Sebastian shouting, "Take that! Now what you got to say?"

Her heart thundered and her pulse raced. She rang the bell, then banged on the front door. "Julian, are you all right?"

First, there was complete quiet. Then heavy footsteps plodded toward the door. The lock turned, and then the door opened. Nyles was standing there, his forehead beaded with perspiration and a pair of boxing gloves in his hand.

"Nyles, what have you done? And what on earth were the four of you thinking, coming here like this? I swear to God, if you've so much as—"

"Hey, sweetheart. Is everything okay?" Julian stepped out of the kitchen.

She leaped into his arms. "Are you all right? I'm sorry about my brothers. I had no idea they were coming here."

"I'm fine, babe. I promise." Julian rubbed a slow circle on her back and kissed her temple. "Were you expecting to find me beaten and tied to a chair?" He chuckled.

"No. *Maybe*." She cradled his cheek and laughed, too. "I wasn't sure what to expect."

"Well, I appreciate the rescue attempt. But your brothers have been here awhile. They could've dumped my body in a back-road ditch by now." His chest rumbled with laughter.

"Hey, it's the thought that counts," she said.

"It is." Julian gazed down at her, his eyes filled with a warmth and affection that made her heart full and her tummy flutter. He lifted her chin. "You know what this means, right?"

"No, what?"

"It means…you care about me. A lot." A warm grin lit his dark eyes. "Like I love you."

"You…*love* me?"

"I do." Julian tucked her hair behind her ear. "My heart belongs to you, Chandra. Now and always."

Tears sprang to her eyes and her chest felt so full she thought it might explode. Chandra wanted to blame her raging hormones. But the truth was so much simpler.

She loved Julian, and she wanted to be with him, too.

Since her return from San Diego, Chandra's heart had been quietly whispering that what she felt for Julian was more than desire or infatuation. It was *love*. She'd just been too afraid to embrace it, fearful of being hurt again.

On the ride to Julian's cabin, she realized she was prepared to go to battle—even with her brothers—to protect the man she loved. The bighearted town doctor with a devastating smile who'd tended to her physical and emotional wounds and helped her mend the pieces of her once-broken heart.

Chandra's eyes filled with tears. "I love you, too."

Julian heaved a quiet sigh of relief and grinned. "You realize I was prepared to take an ass whipping from your brothers, if that's what it took to prove how serious I am about you, Chandra Valentine."

"You were gonna take on all four of my brothers for my hand in marriage?" Chandra couldn't help the euphoria she often felt in Julian's company.

"For you, girl, I would've fought a damn bear."

Julian captured her lips in a kiss that made her tummy flutter and sent heat down her spine.

"Dude, maybe we agreed to bury the hatchet…for now…but she's still my sister." Sebastian frowned, then sipped his imported beer. "I don't need to see this."

For a moment, she'd forgotten about her brothers and all the other cars in the driveway.

"Your poker night. I'm sorry. I completely forgot."

"It's okay." Julian squeezed her hand.

He stepped aside and she could see the two tables filled with familiar faces—many of whom shared her DNA.

"Hi." Chandra gave the roomful of men a small wave. Her cheeks heated with the realization that they'd been privy to their entire conversation. "Sorry to disturb your poker party."

"We needed a chance to regroup." Alonzo pulled out a different brand of imported beer from the cooler. "Your little boyfriend here is whipping our asses."

"Good. That'll save me the trouble." Chandra pointed

a finger at her brother, indicating they'd talk more about this later. "And he's *not* my boyfriend."

Alonzo, Sebastian and Nyles shared puzzled looks while Julian looked wounded.

"He's my fiancé." Chandra's eyes searched Julian's as she squeezed his hand. "If your proposal is still on the table."

"*Yes.* Of course it is," Julian said. He wrapped her up in his arms, lifting her off her feet momentarily. He laughed nervously, fumbling to retrieve something from his pocket.

Julian produced a black ring box imprinted with the logo from Parker's wife Kayleigh's jewelry shop. It was a ring Chandra had admired at the store when she'd visited there several weeks ago. Only the ring had been enhanced since then. The setting and stone were much bigger, befitting an engagement ring.

"Have you been walking around with this ring in your pocket for a week?"

"No." He chuckled as he slid the ring onto her outstretched finger. "Parker delivered it tonight." Julian nodded toward her cousin who was in the midst of cleaning his glasses. "I'd planned to ask you to marry me again in a few days, but this time, I wanted to do it right. Dinner, flowers, a night out, getting down on one knee. Because you deserve that and more."

"That's sweet, Julian. But I don't need any of that." She cupped his whiskered cheek. "I… No, *we*—" she pressed a hand to her belly "—just need you."

He kissed her again.

The sound of clapping and hooting reminded them

they weren't alone, and she reluctantly pulled back from the kiss.

"Jeez, sis, get a room." Alonzo shuddered.

"Or like...*not*," Sebastian countered.

"What did I miss?" Naya huffed, her cheeks reddened by the cold air and her apparent jog. "Is everything okay?"

Julian gazed down at Chandra with a warm smile, his eyes not leaving hers. "Everything is perfect."

"Looks like the doc here will be our future brother-in-law." Nolan sank onto the sofa.

"Which makes him either hella brave or hella crazy." Nyles had strapped on the black-and-red boxing gloves along with a black virtual reality headset. He ducked a right jab from his on-screen opponent on the living room television. "Guess we'll find out which."

"And I guess we know who snitched." Sebastian narrowed his gaze at Naya.

Naya stuck out her tongue, revealing her tongue ring. She wrapped Chandra and Julian up in a hug.

"Congrats, you two." She kissed both of their cheeks. "Welcome to the family, Julian." Naya pressed a hand to Chandra's belly. "I can't wait to be this little muffin's aunt."

Her sister was quickly distracted by the scent of food. She sniffed the air. "Do I smell pastrami? What's the buy-in for this game, anyway? And where's the bathroom? I need to wash my hands before I eat. Never mind—I found it."

Naya was gone before either of them could answer a single one of her rapid-fire questions.

Chandra and Julian both laughed.

"Sorry about my siblings." She glanced around the room. "I feel like I'll be saying that a lot. Are you *sure* you want to do this?"

"I'm positive. They may be...*a lot*." Julian chuckled. "But they obviously care. I was an only kid." He shrugged. "It'll be cool to be part of a big family."

"In a couple of months, when they're all getting on your nerves, I'll remind you that you said that." Chandra pressed another quick kiss to Julian's lips, still slightly in disbelief that they were getting married and having a baby.

It all felt too perfect, just as her previous engagement and all of the perfect wedding plans that went along with it had. Because it was.

From Edward's meticulously orchestrated proposal at the lovely Cheekwood Estate and Gardens, to their elaborate plans for a wedding at The Parthenon in Centennial Park. For months, it had felt like she was floating in some incredible dream, until it'd turned into a nightmare. Just a few weeks shy of her wedding, she discovered her fiancé had rekindled his relationship with his ex.

Julian's proposal hadn't been carefully orchestrated or captured on film. But everything about it *felt* perfect. Like he was the missing piece of her heart that unlocked the fairy-tale love she'd once wanted so desperately. Would it all just blow up in her face again?

"Hey, come with me." Julian led her to his bedroom. They stepped inside and he closed the door. "You okay? Because you look a little..."

"Terrified?" Chandra sank onto the bed. "That's because I am. I know I said I wasn't afraid or overwhelmed by all of this, but that was me lying to myself, not deliberately being dishonest with you."

She was accustomed to walking into a room, taking charge and getting things done. Being in control and delegating. The vulnerability she was feeling now was hard to process.

"I meant what I said about being in love with you. I want to marry you, Julian," she said emphatically. "But you know I was engaged before. On paper, everything seemed picture-perfect. But I was betrayed and humiliated. My entire world imploded." Chandra wiped a finger beneath her eyes and sucked in a deep breath. "I don't know if I can handle another loss like that. You and I, we've already lost so much."

"We have." Julian sat on the bed beside her and threaded their fingers. He kissed the back of her hand. "Maybe that's why I've been afraid to really open up to anyone. But I wasn't expecting you, Chandra. I didn't expect to fall for you. I didn't expect to want a kid or to get married. But with you, I do. And I won't allow fear to make me miss out on the best thing that has ever happened to me."

How was this man so damn amazing?

Julian was an endless source of comfort. A compassionate confidant. A patient suitor. An unselfish lover who seemed to know her body, her needs and desires, even better than she did. He'd been completely open with her. She needed to do the same.

"I'm afraid something will go wrong with this pregnancy," she admitted. "I'm afraid I'll be a terrible mother because I haven't had an example of a good one. That our relationship won't last, and it'll be one more broken marriage in this family. That you'll look at me in a few months when I'm the size of a beached whale and regret this."

Julian's dark eyes seemed to glow with love and understanding. He tightened his grip on her hand. "I know this feels scary, Chandra. But everything is going to be fine—I promise."

She remembered when he'd uttered those very words to her on the plane. Just like then, she realized it was a promise he couldn't keep—even if he wanted to. Still, it felt damn good to hear. "I want to believe that. I *really* do."

"We both know there are lots of things in this life we can't control. But whatever happens, we'll get through it. *Together*. But you should know that I don't have a single doubt about what a great mom you'll be. Because I know you'll be the kind of mother you wished you had. And you're wrong about not having a good example of mothering. From what your brothers have been telling me, you were incredibly nurturing and self-sacrificing. That's why every one of them would run through a brick wall for you. So would I." He stroked her cheek. "Because I love you."

Warm tears slid down Chandra's cheeks. Her heart swelled with affection for this incredible man whom fate seemed to have gift wrapped and hand delivered to her. "I love you too, Julian."

She pressed her lips to his, and his tongue glided against hers.

There was a tap at the bedroom door.

"You realize I was joking when I said get a room?"

"Go away, Alonzo!" they said, simultaneously.

"Y'all got folks out here waiting for y'all. Seems a

little rude." Alonzo's voice grew quieter as his footsteps receded.

"Your brother's right." Julian kissed the shell of her ear. "Can we finish this later?"

"We'd better." Chandra giggled when he kissed the space where her neck and shoulder met.

Julian stood, pulling her into a hug that lifted her off her feet. He set her back down and they returned to the great room, where their family and friends awaited.

Chandra's feet may have been on solid ground, but her heart was soaring.

Maybe this hadn't been the happy ending she'd imagined for herself. But she was excited to begin the next chapter of her life with Julian by her side.

Epilogue

"I now pronounce you husband and wife." The wedding officiant beamed at Julian and Chandra as she placed a hand over her heart. "You may now kiss your bride."

Julian's heart thundered in his chest as the moment settled over him.

Chandra Yvonne Valentine had agreed to be his, and he had promised to be hers. For as long as they both should live.

Julian choked back the tears that clogged his throat. His heart swelled with emotions as he met the gaze of his stunning bride. Her eyes also shone with unshed tears and her almost shy smile made his heart expand uncomfortably in his chest.

Three months ago, Julian couldn't possibly have imagined that he'd be standing here on New Year's Day, newly married, expecting his first child and planning a long-term future in Magnolia Lake with the woman of his dreams.

But here he was. He'd fallen head over heels for Chandra. And now he couldn't imagine life without her.

Julian slipped his arms around Chandra's waist. His lips glided over hers in a kiss that was passionate but sweet.

No matter how many times he kissed Chandra, he could never quite get his fill of those soft, full lips. But this was their wedding, so he'd show some restraint.

"I love you, baby," he whispered so only she could hear him, as the hooting and applause of their friends and family slowly died down.

"I love you, too." Chandra's broad smile made his heart reel.

Julian took her hand. They'd only taken a few steps up the aisle when they were surrounded by their families. First, Julian's mother, looking stunning in her floor-length tan mother-of-the-bride dress, hugged him, then her new daughter-in-law. Next, Chandra's father and sister hugged them both, while her brothers kissed her cheek and shook his hand.

Joe Abbott approached them with a big grin. Julian and Chandra gave the old man a big hug, knowing none of this would've happened if not for him.

Julian glanced around the space that had been a dusty, unused wine-tasting room just two weeks ago. Soon after Chandra had accepted his proposal, they'd planned to get married on New Year's Day in a simple, informal ceremony. She'd wanted to get married at the vineyard, as a symbol of all the good things to come there.

Parker's wife, Kayleigh, had made the engagement ring and their wedding rings.

Naya, Zora, Savannah, Quinn, Julian's mother, and Duke's wife, Iris, had jumped in and helped Chandra find an incredible wedding dress on short notice, arranged the flowers with a local vendor and sourced every other item they'd need. Cole, Julian, Chandra's brothers, Blake, Max, Dallas, and Julian's cousins Elias and Ben helped paint the old place inside and out.

Iris and Savannah had tables, chairs, fairy lights and a host of other decorations brought over from the King's Finest wedding venue barn. Iris and Quinn had baked and decorated the three-tier wedding cake.

Julian couldn't be more grateful for the outpouring of love and support from their friends and family and all the effort they'd put into making their hastily planned wedding both beautiful and memorable.

"I can't believe our families did all this." Chandra smoothed down the skirt of her dress.

The sheer fabric was dotted with crystals that resembled a starry night, especially in the darkened room. A reminder of that first walk around the lake beneath the stars. The V-neck and low-cut back flattered Chandra's curvy frame. And the nude slip beneath the skirt prevented the dress from being too sheer while adding to the ethereal, bohemian aesthetic.

Chandra's wavy sable-brown hair was pulled back in a low, loose chignon, framed by a beautiful halo headpiece Kayleigh created for her. Crystals and freshwater pearls were twisted in a design reminiscent of the grapevines that grew in the vineyards the Valentine family now owned. Her simple makeup enhanced her natural glow.

Julian could barely take his eyes off his wife long enough to survey the room and the people who filled it. He smiled. "I can't believe they were able to make this happen so quickly. You Abbotts are a fierce lot. I pity the soul foolish enough to cross any of you."

"And don't you forget it." Chandra poked a finger in his sternum. Her laugh and soft gaze, filled with love, warmed his chest. She glanced up at him. "I still can't believe this is real."

He understood how she felt. He'd awakened that morning feeling like he was floating on a cloud of bliss. Missing Chandra, since she'd spent the night at the vineyard with her family. But he'd been grateful, knowing her face would be the first one he'd see for the rest of his life.

"Believe it, sweetheart." Julian placed the hand that bore her wedding ring over his heart. He cupped her cheek. "Because I love you, Chandra Valentine-Brandon. And I am so damn lucky to be starting a life and a family with you."

Chandra blinked back the tears that filled her brown eyes. She lifted onto her toes and kissed him.

For a moment, he was lost in her kiss and in the sweet scent of honeysuckle that reminded him of summers when he was a kid and all was right with the world. Before he'd known the pain of grief and loss.

"I wish my dad could've met you. That he'd get to hold his first grandchild." Julian forced a pained smile. "He would've loved you."

"Your dad will always be right here." Chandra pressed

a hand to his heart. "And so will I. I can't wait to make memories of our own here."

Julian gathered his wife in a tight embrace. And for the first time in a very long time, all *was* right with his world again.

* * * * *

Look for the next Valentine Vineyards novel,
coming in spring 2023.

And check out Reese Ryan's
Bourbon Brothers series!
All available now.

Savannah's Secrets
The Billionaire's Legacy
Engaging the Enemy
A Reunion of Rivals
Waking Up Married
The Bad Boy Experiment

#2917 RANCHER AFTER MIDNIGHT
Texas Cattleman's Club: Ranchers and Rivals
by Karen Booth
Rancher Heath Thurston built his entire life around vengeance. But Ruby Bennett's tender heart and passionate kisses are more than a match for his steely armor. Anything can happen on New Year's...even a hardened man's chance at redemption!

#2918 HOW TO CATCH A COWBOY
Hartmann Heirs • by Katie Frey
Rodeo rider Jackson Hartmann wants to make a name for himself without Hartmann connections. Team masseuse Hannah Bean has family secrets of her own. Working together on the rodeo circuit might mean using *all* his seductive cowboy wiles to win her over...

#2919 ONE NIGHT ONLY
Hana Trio • by Jayci Lee
Thanks to violinist Megan Han's one-night fling with her father's new CFO, Daniel Pak, she's pregnant! No one can know the truth—especially not her matchmaking dad, who would demand marriage. If only her commitment-phobic, not-so-ex lover would open his heart...

#2920 THE TROUBLE WITH LOVE AND HATE
Sweet Tea and Scandal • by Cat Schield
Teagan Burns will do anything to create her women's shelter, but developer Chase Love stands in the way. When these enemies find themselves on the same side to save a historic Charleston property, sparks fly. But will diverging goals tear them apart?

#2921 THE BILLIONAIRE PLAN
The Image Project • by Katherine Garbera
Delaney Alexander will do anything to bring down her underhanded ex—even team up with his biggest business rival, Nolan Cooper. But soon the hot single-dad billionaire has her thinking more about forever than payback...

#2922 HER BEST FRIEND'S BROTHER
Six Gems • by Yahrah St. John
Travel blogger Wynter Barrington has always crushed on her brother's best friend. Then a chance encounter with Riley Davis leads to a steamy affair. Will the notorious playboy take a chance on love...or add Riley to his list of heartbreaks?

HDCNM1122

HARLEQUIN
PLUS

Announcing a **BRAND-NEW**
multimedia subscription service
for romance fans like you!

Read, Watch and Play.

Experience the easiest way to get
the romance content you crave.

Start your **FREE 7 DAY TRIAL** at
<u>www.harlequinplus.com/freetrial</u>.